GREED
a life

KEVIN McDERMOTT

THICK
WINTER
PRESS

Greed
A Life

v4.0

ThickWinter Press

ISBN: 979-8-218-80138-0

PRINTED IN THE UNITED STATES OF AMERICA

Also by Kevin McDermott

Fortunes Neck

They Imagine Texas

***Greed:* A life**

For Ellie and Joe.

One's sympathies, of course,
were all on the side of life.

Virginia Woolf
"The Death of a Moth"

It was greed that made him.

The same year Charles Tallack was born a postman in Brooklyn died of isolation. It was 1924. The story was that one day the postman went to the home of a wealthy family with a parcel to deliver. When he rang the bell no one answered. Having delivered the mail at this house for years the postman knew the family went in summer to the Adirondack Mountains for the better air. The butler and his wife would be in their rooms on the fourth floor, the postman presumed, only they were not. They went with their employer to the mountains.

The postman fetched a front-door key kept under a rock in the garden beside the stoop. This was an unlikely thing for the owners of a mansion to do, keep a key under a rock, which makes that part of the story plausible. This is a preposterous universe.

The postman let himself in. The house had a modern electric elevator and the guy stepped into it. He pressed the button and the cab rose about a foot from the floor. Then, nothing. He pressed the button again, click click. He would need to take the stairs instead. But the elevator was designed so that it should never open between floors, for safety. Its door was locked.

What made the postman's story vivid was not the man's starving nor a thirst beyond imagining nor any of that. It was the picture of the postman all alone, waiting his end in that cage suspended a foot from salvation. The light coming and going, passing across the room and then gone from the window again at the end of each day.

Three months later when they came home the family found the man. Horrible for everybody. Amazing that the newspapers could write that the man was thinking this, thinking that. His real thoughts were lost to the past, a hole in the plot.

The postman's story was all over the newspapers before everyone went on to the next thing. Just the way they did about Tallack's father.

All his long life Charles Tallack's worst nightmares were the ones in which he was alone in a small space and unable to get out; even in daylight just thinking this caused him pain in his chest. That feeling of being trapped not physically nor by circumstance merely but by a sensation that would not let go, a feeling that held his heart like a spirit crept in from another world, a spirit who would not speak but did not ever leave him alone.

Tallack's mother was a pretty girl of 19 with a job in an office when she got pregnant. His father, Martin Dempster, was 23. Tallack never knew what Dempster looked like. To his knowledge Tallack never saw a single photograph of the man.

Tallack's mother and Dempster were married in August 1923, Tallack was born in January 1924. In April his mother was granted the annulment of her marriage. After the annulment his mother lived with his Aunt Ruth and the woman Tallack later found out was his grandmother.

Then it was a Friday evening in the hot July of 1924.

When Martin Dempster showed up at Ruthie's apartment that evening, banging on the door, Ruthie told him that Mary had taken the baby out for an airing, out to the grocery. But she let Dempster in; after all, Martin was her brother.

According to what Tallack later found out, Dempster refused to talk to his sister as he waited.

"If I asked even one question," Ruthie told Tallack's Uncle Jimmy later, "Martin would just lift his finger in front of his lips like 'be quiet'. Or he would say 'greed, greed, greed'. Why would he be saying that? He must have flipped his lid."

While Dempster was not talking to Ruthie, Tallack's mother came down the street wheeling the baby in the contraption someone lent her. Ruthie's neighbor from upstairs bumped into them and said Dempster was waiting. Tallack's mother asked the neighbor if he would please go back in and say to Dempster, no, his former wife would not speak with him.

Dempster got that message and ran out into the street to find his baby and its mother. By then they had vanished, out of his life for good he must have supposed. Dempster went back into the apartment house at a run, then up the stairs to the roof. For a good thirty minutes he was up there sitting on the ledge even as his sister Ruthie begged him to come down, please.

Finally Ruthie called the police. They brought a young priest over from St. Rita's, Fr. Cooke; he was pastor there when Tallack was growing up. What Dolan told the newspaper was that he and Dempster were deep in conversation on the roof when Dempster pushed off. From six floors up he died immediately when he hit the ground.

About an hour after this Tallack's mother came back. She had gone to her brother Jimmy's house to drop the baby off. When she found that Jimmy was not at home she had to walk all the way back with her baby—little Tallack—in the carriage. The fire department was hosing off the sidewalk when she returned.

"JILTED PAPA ENDS ALL" said the headline in the bulldog edition of *The Daily News* that evening.

The newspaper story even made a joke about "taking the plunge" in reference to Dempster's marrying Tallack's mother the year before.

Even later no one told Tallack any of this. What he knew about it he acquired on his own and very late in the day. In the meantime, everyone's greed for life went on as it always had. Just as Dempster predicted.

If things are not written down they are missing to history.

Nearly ninety years after being born Tallack was shown a microfiche copy of his birth certificate by his granddaughter Abbie. It looked like a film negative to him. In the very nice handwriting of someone probably dead a long time it was affirmed that Tallack entered this world via Midtown Hospital at 4:43 in the afternoon. If a fact can be neither here nor there that one would be near the top of the list.

The only thing about the birth certificate at all thought provoking was that it listed Tallack under his mother's name, Delroy. Charles Delroy: that would make me someone else, Tallack thought if ever he said that name aloud. Charlie Delroy. It sounded like a name for a bandleader.

If Tallack thought about it, which was close to not at all, he assumed he was legally Dempster's son until the suicide and before Jack Tallack entered the picture. Come to find out, Tallack was wrong.

On his mother's marriage license it said she and Dempster were married in St. Rita's on August 17, 1923. Tallack once worked out the day of the week. It was a Wednesday. Among Catholics the day is the feast of St. Hyacinth, the patron saint of "those who are despised, who are devoid of self-love and who have little sensible consolation."

A Wednesday suggests a small wedding. For a woman at that time to be unmarried and pregnant was far from unknown but still quite a thing for people back then.

Imagine Tallack already on the creep into this life, budding even as his mother said "I do."

Tallack never learned much at all about Dempster, not directly. From his Aunt Connie, Jimmy's wife, Tallack picked up bits and pieces of the world before he came along, but only bits and pieces. Connie said his mother had siblings—his uncle Jimmy and two who died in infancy of one thing and another. Tallack did not remember if she told him what ages they were when they died.

Tallack knew little about his mother's family situation except that her own mother died young and her father lived to a reasonable age for his time. On such points Tallack's mother never had anything to say. The way kids will he got the message to please stop asking please.

Near the end of his life Tallack saw a photograph of his mother at 19, the year she had him. She looks barely more than a girl, pretty and really young in a hobble skirt and cloche hat. It was easy to see what attracted Dempster. But of Dempster there were no photographs. Tallack had only the image in his head of a sorry young man, who maybe touched fire once with the pretty girl from the neighborhood and could not get over it when she went on without him.

How bad do things have to get for someone to leap from a building? Pretty bad, Tallack recognized that. But personally he never felt anything like that impulse. Like anyone else he had glimpses.

There was another man in his mother's life when Tallack was, he could not recollect what he was—12 ,13 years-old?—beginning not to be a little boy anymore. Tallack did not recall having any problems with the guy. He was good for the occasional ice cream or a movie. Without putting it this way to himself, the rest of it was his mother's business. In any case no one was asking Tallack what he thought.

This man—his name was Frank—this man was around more than a little while. He was not some transient. Perhaps the romance with Tallack's mother lasted a year; it is so long ago now. Then one Sunday they were walking home from church and his mother told Tallack out of the blue that Frank had exited the stage.

"It was up to me to decide," she said, or some words close to that, "and what I decide is that I like it better you and me, dear. Frank is a nice man and I hope you will not miss him much but he will not be around anymore."

The two of them were what Tallack was used to, and he did not ever recall being avid for another person to come and live in their house. Still, he felt funny about Frank, bad for him. Maybe that is why Tallack grew up to be Old Faithful as a husband, who knows?

Silence can be alright.

One day in his last winter Tallack was poking in an unlabeled box trying to find his wife's death certificate. He had an idea he needed that piece of paper to do his income tax; God knows why he thought that since he had not worked for income in years. Up on a closet shelf he unearthed a photograph album which he suspected Marie put together because the snapshots from his side of the family have no sort of order, like she had no idea who the people in the photographs were. Half of them Tallack did not know either, though once upon a time he must have.

There was Tallack at about 12 years old, posing with his dukes up and his chin out like Jack Sharkey in his corduroy knickers. Beside that one there was his daughter Maureen showing for the camera what she got for Christmas one year, a cowgirl outfit and a yellow bag; such a fierce small face she had.

Next to these was a photo of Tallack's mother. It showed her sitting in a summer chair beside a lake, a lap blanket hiding her hands. Not quite behind her was that guy Frank. He was not a bad-looking man, dark hair, dark face, big hands that you could see. Already Frank seemed worried, like he knew what was coming. But that was only the effect of looking at photographs when we already know what happens to the people in them.

What really *is* there is the expression on the face of Tallack's mother. She is not ignoring Frank; she has forgotten the guy already. The self-possession pours out, pours out of her.

An expression people use is "I was not born yesterday." But if you were born yesterday all you know is all you have known, if you follow.

All Tallack knew was the two-bedroom apartment on East End Avenue where he lived until the day he married. The apartment was on the first floor of a good building. It was four blocks east from the Third Avenue El, and that is what made it affordable.

Everyone in Yorkville was White. It never occurred to anyone to note this.

The Tallack apartment was down at the end of a long lobby opposite the street entrance. Looking down that hallway one saw people silhouetted behind the smoked glass in the door fishing their pockets for keys. In summer months the lobby and the stairwells had a smell of mothballs. Tallack recalled that smell to the end of his life.

Tallack and his mother had a nice home where the radio was always turned on. But if ever he called that time to mind what Tallack recollected was a silent house. That can't be true but it was his recollection. His mother was solitary. She was friendly to the neighbors, and kind to her son. But you could tell most of the time she was all she needed.

His mother had her brother Jimmy as a sort of counselor. Jimmy and Aunt Connie had a big place seven blocks west on Madison Avenue. They lived there with an unfriendly old lady whose relationship to the household was not clear to Tallack until later, and even then he was not sure. The old lady did not fit the family setup, Tallack could not put his finger on why. Now and then she would say how much she liked children but Tallack did not think so.

This old lady was Tallack's grandmother, his *father's* mother, from the Dempster side. All his life Tallack had only guesses about how she came to live with Jimmy after she had been living with Ruth. Old Mrs. Dempster was a hard person—armored—or perhaps that was just the way a child took her in.

For one reason and another Jimmy and Connie had no children of their own. All day Connie and the old lady were left to themselves. After school Tallack used to go there while his mother was at work—"out to business" people used to call it. Uncle Jimmy was a lawyer, and he acted like a father to Tallack's mother, probably because that job was vacant. Jimmy was older than she was by a few years. He was the kind of guy always needling, always teasing when he talked—his way of showing he was boss. When he did this to his mother Tallack hated him.

For no reason that anyone ever told him Tallack started kindergarten a year later than most of the kids. At about ten years old he convinced his mother that he was reliable enough to see himself home after school in the afternoons. After that he did not have to kill the hours with Aunt Connie and the old lady until his mother returned.

Expectation is in tension with preparations for departure.

In 1941 Tallack graduated high school at 17 years old. That summer he got a job at Orbach's department store in Union Square. It was in merchandising, about which you can imagine how much he knew. They paid him $28 a week, excellent money for a kid like he was then. Orbach's was hoping he might make a career there. Pearl Harbor happened in December and the next July Tallack was drafted.

In between he met Marie Brochain.

Marie worked on the expectant-ladies floor with her friend Barbara Riordan. Barbara worked for pocket money while she waited for somebody or other to marry her. But Marie was a girl with ambitions. She made her own clothes and took seriously the debates in the women's magazines—hemlines and hats, gloves or no gloves. To everyone else she was just one more girl with an interest in clothes. But in secret Marie dreamed of being one day a big shot in fashion.

In a later age a woman like Marie Brochain would have

had nothing to do with Charles Tallack, and he always knew it.

The thing to keep in mind is that when Tallack met Marie he had no idea what he wanted from this life, not even how to put the question to himself. For him in that sense the Second World War was timely.

World history will bias the course of anybody's life, for those who aren't destroyed by it, obviously.

The future invents itself without our help.

When Charles Tallack married Marie Brochain his mother assumed Marie had never had anyone explain the birds and the bees to her. Tallack's mother was right more or less, though Marie had worked it all out by the time she met Tallack.

Marie's father had not been able to bring himself to talk to either of his children about such a thing. The few times it came up Mr. Brochain referred obliquely to *relations*. In girlhood this term made Marie picture a writhing bed full of aunts, uncles and cousins.

For the most part Marie's father passed the job of explaining relations to his sister, Marie's Aunt Mae. After Marie's own mother died Mae was a part-time mother to Marie and her older brother Edward. She had three daughters older than Marie so she had been through the whole thing.

Until the year Mae and her husband Frank bought a house in Queens she was living upstairs from the Brochains at their place in the Bronx.

Aunt Mae would say to Marie, "Tell me about your boyfriends, darling." This had the advantage of sounding like an invitation to gossip. It was a smart way to go about it. With his own kids later Tallack tried to remember the technique.

Once Marie told Aunt Mae about a girl at her school who had a boyfriend and got pregnant. The nuns threw her out. Marie did not know how to say so, but for a while she worried having a boyfriend at all could make a girl pregnant. She told Aunt Mae about the girl, and Aunt Mae seemed worried to hear about it. "It is a long life," was the only comment she made. Whatever you do, in other words, think about tomorrow. At least Marie got the message to be prudent.

The first time Tallack and Marie ever had relations she was happy. It was the evening Mrs. Tallack had the Brochains to dinner. They had been at the window of Mrs. Tallack's bedroom watching a summer storm pass through New York, so it was romantic. Traffic noise shushed on the wet street out the window, fresh wind ruffled the curtains.

"Who's this guy?"

Marie was holding the framed photo Mrs. Tallack kept on the vanity. The metal frame was all gone green. Tallack liked knowing the word for this green: *verdigris*. All his life Tallack took pleasure in knowing the right word. In general it is not a useful trait.

"My father."

"You must take after your mother."

Marie relaxed her weight against Tallack and they tumbled back onto his mother's bed, which was thrilling. They were young, pleased, pleased the way anyone is the first time they do something important; and of course they were giddy with the sex.

"Ummm," she said. This drew the actual breath out of Tallack's lungs. "Gimme a little kiss, will ya, huh?"

Later, spectacular in his old age, Tallack could not forget it. "Gimme a little kiss, will ya, huh?" Marie sounded like the hungriest woman in the world. And it was *him* she wanted to eat. He always remembered her waxy red lipstick, which women do not wear anymore like that.

They may have been hoping for a baby right that minute; the government would have drafted Tallack anyway. Marie's body radiated heat he could feel through the cotton of her slip. She looked him over, probably searching behind his eyes for second thoughts, of which he had none; she had winced a little. Then Marie said something that did not necessarily follow.

"I feel bigger," which pleased Tallack and he kissed her again. And not just a peck either.

Marie put on the pretty peach dress she bought special to wear that evening. She was gorgeous. It was killing him. You can see why all this stuck deep in Tallack's memory.

"Bank's closed, buddy," Marie told him when he kissed her again.

Marie and Tallack were at work cutting vegetables when his mother returned home from her job in a Brooklyn office. On that hot evening it was a wintertime meal she had planned, a formal meal. Into the pot roast they cut carrots and chopped onions.

Tallack knew how ill at ease his mother was if called upon to be a host. Mrs. Tallack's idea of entertaining was to fix the most amount of food she could afford and feed it to her guests, and to make sure there was liquor enough. There was an uncertainty in her that some mistook for being stern. His mother never learned a sense of ceremony—who the hell was around to teach it to her? She was tense with the effort of maintaining her dignity—widowed, worried over money all the time and all the rest of the things Tallack in time found out.

Tallack put dinner plates on the table and laid ashtrays around. This was life, this was ordinary life.

Mrs. Tallack set one of the paper grocery bags on the kitchen table. A can of asparagus tips tumbled out and thunked on the linoleum. Before that evening Tallack never saw a can of asparagus tips.

"What do you do with these, ma?"

"Serve them for appetizers, I think. What does it say on the can?"

"Just says how tasty they are. That is their word for it: 'tasty.'"

"Shave your face, Charles. You look like a bum."

"Scratchy-face," Marie said.

In the bathroom shaving Tallack listened for any trouble coming from the kitchen. "How long till they're done?" he heard Marie ask. She meant about the Brussels sprouts boiling around in a pot.

"Oh dear," Mrs. Tallack told her, "they aren't near ready. You wait until they stop bouncing and sink to the bottom. That's how you know." In those days this was how people cooked.

From the hall closet Tallack dragged out the bridge table. Sometimes if Uncle Jimmy came over they might play blackjack to indulge him.

Mrs. Tallack said she forgot to get ice for the whiskey.

"Be a lamb," she said to Tallack, "and go down the deli to get us a bag of ice. Marie's father will be wanting a drink when he gets here."

"Pop never touches it," said Marie. "His father died of drinking. I have an Uncle Raymond who every time someone mentions alcohol he spits."

Mrs. Tallack lifted her chin. She had spent good money for liquor.

"The others'll want a drink, at least," she said. "Go around and get the ice, Charles."

Later Marie told Tallack he was not out the door three minutes when his mother asked, "What has your father told you about wedded life, Marie?" They were standing at the stove.

"What what's like?"

"Wed. Ed. Life."

"What do you mean? Getting along and everything?"

"Yes, that, and the children. Has your father ever spoken to you about it?"

Marie was on the edge of responding, "We don't have children" when she realized that Mrs. Tallack got her alone because she meant to have a talk. She had sent Tallack out to the delicatessen to get ice so that she could do her duty by this motherless girl.

The kitchen was humid with the thick smell of the sprouts cooking and pot roast. Through the window there was a bit of a breeze and the lull of traffic down in the street. The noises of people having their dinners drifted out all the open windows of Yorkville. Little dramas everywhere. Marie was sure she heard the silverware of families having dinner just suddenly stop so they could listen.

Summertime. Urban summertime. So promising.

"The object of marriage," Mrs. Tallack was explaining to Marie, meaning the object of the marriage bed, though perhaps not, who knows? The lid on the pot of Brussels sprouts began to ring, boiling over. The two women leapt to their feet to save dinner, glad to break the tension.

"Marie, you're bleeding!"

"Cripes!"

The peach dress Marie bought only that week was ruined. Tears started in her eyes. Mrs. Tallack said, "It always comes at the worst possible time. Don't I know. Here, step out of that."

Mrs. Tallack ran a sink of cold water in the bathroom and put the dress to soak, when really what was the point?

"Everyone will see it there when they come," Marie moaned.

"Don't worry about what everyone will see," which was the right thing to say but not much help.

Mrs. Tallack loaned Marie a dress of her own, a candy-striped number with a low-slung waist and a hobble skirt.

The hem hung six inches below the knee. The sash was too tight around the waist, the shoulders binding under Marie's arms. She looked like a poorly wrapped gift.

Marie looked at herself in the mirror of Mrs. Tallack's vanity. An hour before she had found herself beautiful. Now she looked like a hobo.

Meanwhile Tallack knew nothing.

Tallack was coming back from the deli with the chopped ice when he met the Brochains. Marie's father and her brother Edward wore identical blue suits; until Tallack noticed the fedora Mr. Brochain carried in his left hand he mistook them for cops. Without glasses Tallack's eyesight was always poor. With glasses Tallack was fine.

Aunt Mae was in a white dress patterned with cabbage roses. Owing to the shoulder pads in that dress Mae looked formidable, small as she was. Mae was a bit heavy, though not in a completely unattractive way. Frank, her husband, was in his tan seersucker, the suit he wore in summer. Frank probably did not weigh more than Mae. Frank was a fireman, so thin his Adam's apple stuck out like a goiter, and a face so red you would think he just came from a three-alarm blaze; he was a good man but he could be impatient. Mae's face always seemed flushed too. They must have been a passionate pair.

The four of them walked up from East End Avenue in the cherry red light of the dying sun. The afternoon rain left the air sticky.

Mr. Brochain said, "Warm night." He brushed the stiff gray hair on his head with the palm of his hand. Absently he wiped the sweat on his pants leg.

"What do you think of my new lid, Charles? I bought it for Saturday. It's hot on my head." Mr. Brochain looked at that new hat like it might be defective.

Edward shaved for the big dinner and got his hair cut. This was encouraging because sometimes Edward forgot those things. Edward's hair was nearly all gone gray like his father's. At this time he was about 25 years old.

"Nervous about Saturday?" Edward asked Tallack.

"What's to be nervous?"

"That's the boy, Charles," Mae told him. "So far you're doing well with this family."

At the apartment Tallack discovered he had no keys. He pressed the ivory button next to the lobby door. His mother was a long time buzzing them in. At the end of the foyer she stood waiting.

"Come in, come in," she said, welcoming as she knew how.

Mrs. Tallack took the men's jackets and complimented Mae on her pretty dress. Like Mrs. Tallack Mae compensated for the disadvantages of being short and a woman with energy in the way she moved, energy that felt like defiance; apart from that the two women were different as chalk and cheese.

Tallack was hoping Mae's warmth would make his mother feel a success—even as he sensed his mother was irritated with Mae for bringing potato salad. It was meant to be a friendship offering; Mae was famous for potato salad. Tallack worried his mother would interpret it as a comment on her ability to provide.

"Come in and sit down please. What's everyone having?" All the Brochains drank scotch but Marie's father, who liked just seltzer. "Coming up. Charles—did you bring the ice?" Before he could answer his mother took the package out of his arms and was gone to the kitchen.

"Where's your bride to be, Charles?" Frank asked Tallack.

"Mother, what did you do with Marie?"

"Keep your shirt on!"

"I know that voice," Mr. Brochain said, but under his breath.

"Hello, everyone." Marie had materialized. She had her hands clasped over her stomach in a funny way, like a man fond of his potbelly. That dress she has on is different, Tallack thought.

"What happened to the peach job you were wearing?"

"I changed it."

Mrs. Tallack came from the kitchen with highballs, everything on ice. She carried the glasses on a Chinese lacquer tray decorated with a fire-breathing dragon that came down from her father.

Mr. Brochain made a toast, the toast of a man uncomfortable making toasts.

"To Charles and Marie. May the marriage flourish."

"Amen," said Edward the way someone would after a prayer. And they all drink.

Over dinner Mrs. Tallack made a point of speaking with Edward, out of politeness. With his badly cut gray hair and smiling face Edward seemed content merely being in attendance.

"What is it you do, Edward?"

"These days?"

"Yes."

"Before long I'll be following Charles into the service, or that's the assumption. Either that or I'll be the most eligible bachelor in New York."

"They're scouring the streets for young men," said Mae.

Even in the atmosphere of emergency, when every man under 30 who could draw breath was called up, no one really thought Edward would be drafted; it was one of those stories a family tells itself. Edward was called by his draft board for a physical and classified but they did not follow up. They must have sensed that Edward surrendered easily and that would have been demoralizing to the other men.

Until Mr. Brochain died he lived with Edward, two womenless men. Their housekeeping was a catastrophe; we needn't say more than that.

Frank told Edward, "Don't you worry. Your father and I will be here watching the coasts." Like a lot of men Frank was touchy about being left home when he still had the fight left in him. "That right, Gerry?" he said to Marie's father.

"We'll keep an eye on things." Mr. Brochain was enjoying the pot roast.

"I wish the war could end tomorrow," Marie put in. She was in a sour mood about everything. "Charles calls it an adventure. I don't know the Corrigans were so happy to see Danny go." Danny Corrigan lived upstairs from the Brochains and was killed in the Coral Sea the pervious spring. So because of Danny Corrigan Marie looked up accusingly at Tallack. All heads turned in his direction.

"That is not what I said." Tallack dragged a fat glass ashtray across the table and lit a cigarette.

"Don't smoke at the dinner table, Charles," his mother said. He stubbed the cigarette out, careful not to break it for later.

"The other evening with Danny's father I walked home from the subway," said Mr. Brochain, chewing on a piece of meat. "You could barely get a word out of him. Poor man looks like a ghost." Mr. Brochain stopped short and looked at Tallack. For the first time it occurred to him that having his daughter marry a guy going to war was not the best thing.

Tallack felt the mood shifting against him. He did not know what he had done to cause this.

"I'm going to get a safe job away from all the noise," he said, "We'll be at this table a year from now—although I know that may be a disappointment to some of you." This last line Tallack added with a sweeping glance at the Brochains. They pretended to laugh, recognizing that they may have been upsetting Mrs. Tallack.

Tallack's mother got on like a house afire with the Brochains. Everyone came to the occasion wishing it to be so.

"Wonderful supper, Mary," said Mr. Brochain. Mrs. Tallack went pink with pleasure. Unequivocal praise was not in her tradition. Mr. Brochain undid the top button of his trousers.

By the end of the evening even Marie brightened up. For dessert there was coffee and a chessboard cake from the baker. Aunt Mae wrote the recipe for her potato salad on two cards, one for Mrs. Tallack and the other for Marie. Mrs. Tallack would never make it but in the years to come Marie often did. Even Tallack liked it enough to learn how after Marie died.

And they played cards, which Tallack knew was a satisfaction to his mother.

Crowds amplify a predisposition to loneliness.

Tallack married on a Saturday in September 1942. The church was hot and the noise of the big floor fans filled the church, making the vows hard to hear.

Tallack's mother and his Uncle Jimmy and Aunt Connie were there. The Brochains were there too, of course, but Marie's people were mainly in Boston, and with the war they did not travel much. It was not that they couldn't, they just did not.

They dispensed with all the bride's side/groom's side business; everyone mixed in, Tallack's mother between Mr. Brochain and Edward. His mother was light-hearted that day, which she was not always.

Tallack did basic training in Georgia in just 60 days. He was back in New York for three days in the week before Thanksgiving. Marie and he spent those nights at the Shelton Hotel.

Someplace there is a picture of Tallack taken by Marie

on the morning he sailed for Europe. He is in the Shelton's lobby wearing his dress uniform, fatigue cap folded over his belt, stiff-armed, beaming. He looks pretty good.

He was nineteen years old.

From the Shelton Tallack went on the Hudson & Manhattan Railroad to Hoboken with several other guys he was friendly with by force of circumstance. Marie went uptown by subway to collect his mother.

Tallack waited for them in the Hoboken terminal under a big red **T** in the hall. Next to the hall the Queen Mary was tied up, waiting to take the soldiers to England.

The place was jammed, of course. In the heat and the smoke and the roar of a thousand voices Tallack stood under his **T**.

Flags in the rafters, giant suspended advertising cards—cigarettes, laxatives, chewing gum, Plymouths. Old men selling peanuts. Red Cross ladies handing out coffee and cider. An army band playing. The *point* of everything seemed to be the creation of commotion, to distract everyone.

The hour of sailing was for some reason a secret—how would a big ship sneak out of New York harbor without anyone noticing? Soldiers were supposed to board at three but at 2:30 Marie and Tallack's mother were still not there, lost in all the foot traffic snarling the narrow streets around the docks.

There was a tiny pile of Chesterfields at Tallack's feet by the time they made it. He was a little peevish at being kept waiting and did not want to be.

"I thought I wouldn't get to say so long," Tallack said.

No sooner did they arrive than some whistle blew so loudly it hurt the ears.

The roar of voices changed tone to something louder and higher pitched. Marie made things worse by starting to cry and hanging herself from around Tallack's neck. It was probably for the best that they did not have more time, now he thought about it.

Tallack's mother held her purse with both hands and looked at him—greedily, he thought.

Tallack wrapped his arms around her. Her head barely reached his breastbone. This was the last day he saw his mother alive.

"Life can be good. Then you lie down, and stare up at the ceiling and the sadness falls on you."

Robert Frank

There is no cure for solitude.

More than two and a half years Tallack was gone. The first few months away the separation from home bothered him. In situations like that no one stops missing the old life. After a while we become accustomed to its absence. We are busy, and that is how to get by.

The Army Air Force assigned Tallack to the quartermaster corps, so in the end he spent the war driving trucks. That had him on the move all the time, transporting loads from the docks in Liverpool and Plymouth to bases all over the south of England and the Midlands. It was fine.

Tallack fell into the routine of the job, chasing up and down the countryside from one airbase to another in supply convoys. To be honest he enjoyed it. The army did not ask much of him, and he never had so much independence before in his life. The war made Tallack feel not more grown up but more young.

Tallack got used to the war, to the taste of danger always underneath everything. No, not danger—a mood of suspense, something new in his life. He was aware of it all the time, a tightness just at the place where his ribs joined.

Tallack never got closer to France than the Dover cliffs. The cliffs were an excursion he made on one of his days off with Cynthia Hipsley and Syd Ballard. Cynthia was seconded from the staff of some Royal Navy commodore for reasons of bureaucracy or diplomacy that even she had a hard job explaining. Syd and she helped with special deliveries they made for the first time in the winter of 1943.

Syd was a big guy, a Royal Marine, a Londoner with curly hair and a thin mustache and for such a large man a surprisingly small voice. He liked to sing.

I've just returned to England, from somewhere overseas
Instead of love and kisses, the girls gave me the breeze
Said they preferred the Yanks and gum
A little jeep, a country run
My good-time English sweetheart
My faithless English Rose

Syd was at times tiresome. He needled Tallack about "lorry" versus "truck," and had a steady stream of wisecracks about an America in his head where everyone was rich (he liked to pretend Tallack had oil wells in Oklahoma). But Cynthia liked that song of his about English girls, probably because it was about somebody else. She was wed to a soldier, a Tommy named Bert, though Tallack kept thinking Tommy was his actual name. At the beginning of the war Bert was captured in North Africa. It seemed like Cynthia was yearning for him. It was not so simple as that.

In the buildup to the invasion of France the three of them began delivering something secret: mustard gas, tons of it before they were done. After the war Tallack did not even tell Marie, not certain if he was still expected to keep this secret. The gas was wanted in case the invasion went wrong and something drastic needed to be done.

Whoever decided these things wanted the deliveries to be inconspicuous, so the three of them worked apart from the big convoys, which to Tallack only felt more conspicuous but no one was asking him. After a while they considered it a cushy job, driving around and talking about all sorts of things, the three of them smoking like mad, oblivious to the cargo sitting right behind them in the truck. The times made them reckless, the times and the being young.

Syd and Cynthia never tried of teasing Tallack about his American way of speaking. They loved hearing him pronounce his soft New York *r's.*

"Say *here,* Charlie."

"Say *heart.*"

"Say *father.*"

By the end of his life Tallack had erased the New York quality in his *r*'s. It was just time that did it.

Around the time Paris was liberated Syd said to Tallack, "You know, forgive me saying so but I'm a bit sad about it, Charlie boy. The thing'll be over soon, and they'll send us home. I've liked being a soldier, Charlie. I shall miss it, and I'll tell you that for nothing." Syd's eyes were brimming.

Tallack worried about going home too, when he thought about it, although he told everyone—told himself—how much he missed home and Marie.

Between Syd and Tallack there was no competition for Cynthia or anything like that. To begin with they were all married and Syd made endless jokes about what a good Methodist he was. Cynthia was not pretty in the usual ways, but Tallack found her attractive. She had something—an elegance in her long face, one of those strong Saxon faces—a good nose. Tallack always liked a fine nose.

What got him, what got him more than anything, was Cynthia's copper-colored hair. It was a tangled bronze that went every which way if the weather was damp, and in England this was most of the time. There was some connection to Marie's red hair, perhaps. But Marie had a little nose—like Myrna Loy, Tallack used to think—and a heart-shaped face. And Cynthia was much taller than Marie, really as tall as Tallack and for a man Tallack was of average height.

Easily the sharpest memory of the war for Tallack was a run to Plymouth a few weeks after Normandy. The war still had a long way to go but he could feel the end coming.

They were driving back from an airfield in Kent without Syd. His kid fell down a full flight of stairs at school and broke his arm seriously. Syd got compassionate leave to go up to London for a few days. They were going back empty so being short-handed did not matter.

Tallack and Cynthia stayed over at the airbase. In the morning he drove to the women's guesthouse to collect her. She came out on the porch in fatigues, blouse untucked, hair still wet from a shampoo; Tallack loved the memory of this to the last day of his life.

"Good morning, sunshine," Cynthia said. At that she bent over, grabbed her thigh with both hands and shook her head, shook her head the way a big dog would if it got wet. The sky was so empty and blue it made Tallack feel an ache.

The whole rest of that day with Cynthia Tallack could smell her scent in the cab of the truck. They went the long way back to London because they were expected to keep away from the main roads.

They were still well to the east of Epping Forest when a V-1 fell barely a quarter mile in front of them. It came down so close they felt the shock wave but not so near that they saw the flash. The rocket fell square on a house—what are the odds of that?—blasting rubble and furniture across the road. Who knows what a rocket was doing so far east of London? That was the unnerving thing about the V-1s—they come down anywhere. There was a fire and the front of someone's house down and things in the road. The truck could not go through.

A cop directed them into an orchard for the night. He directed Tallack to a working callbox so he could telephone the dispatcher at High Wycombe. The guy at the other end was an idiot Scot whom Tallack knew slightly and who made the predictable remarks about spending the night with Cynthia.

Whatever else you want to say about them the majority of men are dopes when it comes to women, as Tallack would later instruct his granddaughters. It is never too soon to figure this out.

In the sky and all at once little Halifax's and four-engine Lancasters appeared in clumps of four and five, condensation trails way up in the starry night, another world up there, the air back on earth vibrating with the flyers navigating in the thin atmosphere.

"That is a nice sound, isn't it?" The airplanes, Cynthia meant.

"Not if you're German."

"They've got it coming. Too bad for them."

Tallack, sitting at the wheel looking out on an orchard, smelling apples, or maybe he imagined that. He loved the insect racket and sugary smells that come off a field on a summer night; he was pretty happy. With the war and all and far from everything and someone's house still burning, who knew if anyone was home when it happened, Tallack sat thinking this was the best time he would ever have in his life. What a thing to think, but he was a kid.

"My sister Barbara builds those Lancasters," Cynthia said. "She works at Avro's in Manchester."

In a little while Tallack noticed Cynthia was asleep. Cynthia did that comical thing where the sleepy person keeps falling against you, canting over like a chopped tree. Each time Tallack shrugged her upright and back into place.

At last Tallack was sleepy too and did not shrug. Anyway it was cozy having Cynthia rest against him—not just because she was a woman, which given everything should have been enough, but because she was Cynthia.

Mainly Tallack's thoughts were innocent until Cynthia slipped her hand over his. For a woman she had a big hand. This was Tallack's first impression.

"This is my birthday, Charlie. I'm 24."

"Happy birthday."

"Makes me melancholy, having a birthday."

"You must be missing Tommy."

"Bert."

"Bert."

"I'm not. It is the having another birthday."

"We both have a few years to go before we start saying things like that."

"Already I feel old and tiresome, Charlie. There's no excitement in life."

"Earlier we had a rocket blow up a house—that's not enough excitement for you? I can still smell the fire."

"This will end. I mean the life to come. Bert will make it home, God willing. We'll be young for a few more years and then that will be that. The most it will ever be is pleasant."

"Maybe."

Cynthia slid across his lap so that he was talking down into her ear. Years later he would be soothing his kids and when they lay across his legs that way it instantly brought Cynthia to mind, how he went on supporting her hand even after his right arm lost all sensation, her hair with its shampoo'd smell.

"No maybes, Charlie. It is too soon to feel this way. About that you are right."

Fortunately for his paralyzed arm but sad for Tallack overall Cynthia sat herself up and leaned into the door on her side of the cab.

"It grieves me that I married Bert. Every day it grieves me. Are you shocked?"

"No. You're honest."

"My father, he was the one. Bert is his friend Mac's stepson. The pair of them thought if we tied the knot it would tidy things up."

"Why did you go along with it?"

"Perfectly well I know why. To get free of him."

"Your father?"

"My father."

"But you did what he wanted."

"We were 19. We were not very smart."

"Bert too?"

"Bert felt the same way I did. For him getting married was a way to turn the tables over, kind of, live his own life."

"Home we say 'kick over the traces'."

"I think we say that here too. Is it something to do with horses?"

"Must be. It sounds exhilarating, like I imagine it would feel to ride a horse."

"Do you know, I've never been on a horse."

"Me neither."

"We wanted that, to feel exhilarated, to do something bold. Bert and I went out for a summer, and for just a moment I thought I was up the duff. I was mistaken but it got us to the registry office. I'll bet money that Bert, wherever he is tonight, is telling this same story to someone."

"Is it his birthday too?"

Cynthia laughed. This always made Tallack feel like a success with women, although little did he know. Over her shoulder out the window in the field he saw something moving. The silhouette was simultaneously shiny and dark, both at once the way soot is, both at once.

"Was he mad?"

"How d'you mean? Crazy?"

"Was Bert mad that you weren't going to have a baby? Angry."

"No, he was *for* the idea of being married, like I said. Thinking I was in the pudding club, to quote my proper mother, was the push he was looking for. I don't think I ever liked Bert better than I did the day we were talking about quitting the marriage. Then it seemed like the next day he was mobilized. And what woman wants to be known for un-marrying a departing soldier?"

"None that I know." Tallack's eye kept going to the shiny thing moving in the field, idly, back and forth like someone pacing.

"I'm terrible, Charlie. My first thought when I heard Bert was captured was 'now I'm for it, I'll never get out of this box'."

"Who called you terrible? And you never know what the future holds."

"That is not very clever, Charlie."

"It is the best I've got."

"This is awkward, Charlie, but I need to visit the ladies."

"At this hour I don't know where you're going to find one. Oh, of course."

Cynthia left an almost touchable imprint in the space where she had sat.

While she was gone Tallack was free to restore the circulation in his arm and look hard at the dark thing moving in the field. He fished his eyeglasses out of his shirt pocket and peered. It was more shine than shadow, as if polished—like anthracite, say. Whatever it was moved haphazardly, as if it bouncing into something and then trying another way forward.

Tallack looked through the windscreen and noticed a white speck the size of his thumbnail. Splatter of some type. On a second look he realized he was looking at the half moon, bright in the violent sky.

Cynthia returning stepped up into the cab and continued to Tallack's lips. It was not a passionate kiss; more like actors kissing in the movies. Still, she did it, that was enough. She came back to the truck meaning to do it.

"Hold on to me," she said. "You may be the last man besides Bert who ever holds me. Hold me on my birthday, Charlie."

"Many happy returns, Cyn."

After that you might presume that Tallack had a hard time sleeping. You would presume wrong. He slept well. It was a bad dream that woke him. A man was coming for him. There was something in the man's hands, but whatever it was he had his back turned away to hide it. Tallack charged him, swinging his fists and half knocking himself to the floor of the cab.

"All right?" Cynthia spoke from inside her sleep.

"The sky is brightening," Tallack replied. "Maybe we can get on our way soon."

At the far edge of the field two men loaded a wain they were filling with green hay. Their horse shuffled in its traces, back and forth.

Mourning infiltrates the lives of everyone.

One day not long after these things happened Tallack was writing to Marie about getting stranded with Cynthia.

Cynthia hails [who uses a word like "hails" except in a letter when they are trying to sound like a person writing?] *from Manchester and in the worst days of the 'blitz' she was still civilian. (Her husband was captured at Cyrenaica and it was after that happened she went on to join the army.) Four years ago they got it really bad up there, when Cynthia was still living with her family. Sitting on our 'sidetrack' the other night she looked up the road at the wreck and said it reminded her of those days. She told me that when the sirens went her mother used to put on a hat and get her purse before she would go out and lie in the Anderson shelter they had in their backyard, which Cynthia said was always full of water. If they ever have an air-raid in Yorkville I can see my mother doing something like that!*

In fact Tallack could not see his mother doing something like that; he was only making a rhetorical flourish in a letter, as people do.

Marie had Tallack's letter with her at work the day after it arrived. She decided Mrs. Tallack would get a kick out of hearing herself compared to the Mancunians. On an impulse she took the Third Avenue elevated to 79th Street that evening. It was early summer and what else did Marie have to do?

Midway down the block she spotted Tallack's mother out in front of her apartment house talking with a man in a white summer hat. From the enthusiasm in the way Mrs. Tallack said hello Marie knew at once that she was glad to be saved from this guy. You can always tell.

The man was Mr. Feld from Mrs. Tallack's office. Mr. Feld lived around the corner over on East End Avenue. It was his habit every evening to walk Mrs. Tallack to her door; it was Mrs. Tallack's fate to be walked. Mr. Feld would bend her ear. The previous summer his wife passed away of something protracted. Although Mr. Feld was younger than Tallack's mother he was married 14 years. He had no children and he missed the wife who died.

"The poor man has only two things to talk about," said Mrs. Tallack after Feld was gone. "Either something reminded him of his wife the other day or what does it all mean. If you ask me he does himself harm." She invited Marie inside for cold supper.

"What was the wife's name?" Marie asked. Marie was

trying to show interest.

"God forgive me," said Mrs. Tallack, "he's said it a hundred times and I can't remember." And they laughed out loud.

> *I should have felt mean laughing at Mr. Feld, but I think your mother really feels for him at heart. Because she has made her mind up to live with things the way they are, hasn't she?—she is like the old lady in the bomb shelter you wrote me about in your letter. The way she is I think it is amazing Mr. Feld doesn't make her more impatient. I'd have made my annoyance at him pretty obvious a long time ago—you know that, don't you? I guess your mother needs the job, though, so she can't be telling her boss to go get lost.*
>
> *Come home and camp on my doorstep, handsome.*

Tallack always wanted to meet Mr. Feld but he never did. In his mind Tallack credited Mr. Feld with the friendliness that developed between his mother and Marie that summer.

Soon they were meeting almost once a week—for church and breakfast on Sunday, for shopping on Saturday. They turned out to be girls of a feather, city women who took for granted that they were all wised up. They often spoke on the telephone. One Sunday Mr. Brochain and Edward joined them for a picnic in Central Park. The next day Marie wrote to Tallack that on their way home Marie's brother Edward remarked that Mrs. Tallack struck him as "a woman who finds life's mysteries unimpressive."

> *It is not surprising you're a lot of what we talk about, Charles—you're 'our boy', after all. (I think we find this very*

satisfying when all is said and done!) These days we are very friendly and I have found myself feeling 'mothered'. I hope she would not mind my saying that. (The other night going off to sleep I had a funny picture in mind of your mother married to Pop. If Pop only knew half the things I thought would be an improvement for him! He's too old for her.)

Wednesday night we went to a movie together—'When the Wind Blows', a good comedy we both liked.

On Mrs. Tallack's last birthday she wrote to her son in England about speaking to Marie on the telephone.

Dear Charles,

Sunday evening I spoke to your bride. She sounds well and is always very busy at her job. Mr. Brochain came on and we said hello. This week I have a bit of a chest cold and he very kindly asked how I was feeling. He "waxed" very funny on the subject of illness, which is a subject only we "old folks" find humor in. I have a suspicion he may be lonely by himself with just Ed. and Marie for company, who need to lead their own lives after all. He is always so kind on the telephone and is just like Marie in his good nature and his talkativeness.

That same summer Mrs. Tallack fell sick with pneumonia. To look after her Marie moved into Tallack's boyhood bedroom on East 79th Street and went to work every day from there.

Tallack's Aunt Ruth helped during the day. (At the time Tallack still thought Ruthie was his cousin.) Mr. Feld offered his help too. (One evening Marie had the idea of asking Mr.

Feld to walk Ruthie up the street to the Third Avenue el. Nothing came of it.) Marie wrote that Ruthie was efficient and when she was around made herself useful, but Mr. Feld was trouble. The distress in his face when he was with Mrs. Tallack made Marie leery of letting him in the front door; seeing the shade of the late Mrs. Feld, no doubt.

Mainly it was Marie with Mrs. Tallack, and dire though the situation was Marie wrote to Tallack that they were content with each other.

The pneumonia gained on Mrs. Tallack and in July she died, never knowing when her son was coming home or if he came home at all. It had to be one of the hardest things Marie ever did in her life up to that point writing to Tallack after his mother passed away.

> *The only thing I would want to say first is that your mother was not in pain. It has been hot here because it is July, and your mother ran a fever most of the time (except when she would suddenly turn very cold, scaring me silly) so that was very uncomfortable for her. But no pain. We've all been working shifts the last two weeks to take care of her—me, Ruthie, Jimmy & Connie, Edward, my father. Pop was the one in her room when she passed. It was about five in the morning and he was asleep in that nice wing-back chair beside her bed. Something woke him, some sound he heard, and when he looked at your mother he knew. I was asleep in your room and pop called to me. Your mother had a look on her face like she was about to wake up from a nice dream but could not quite get up there all the way. I took that for a good sign of how she was feeling at the very end.*
>
> *We waked her in a dress she asked for specifically. A*

week or more ago when she suddenly got really sick she said to me "when they lay me out please put me in that one." I did not want her talking that way and I told her to stop the joking. I knew the dress she meant—an old one with a hobble skirt she leant me that time I had the 'accident' when everyone was coming to dinner which it still embarrasses me to mention. I hope she knows in heaven that I came through for her.

I did not know if there was a priest she liked to say the Mass. Jimmy told me to ask for Fr. Dolan, who was all right; don't know if you ever met him. Jimmy, Connie, Ruth, her mother, Mr. Feld (who cried the most of any of anybody, for a man anyway), Edward & my father were there. Uncle Frank was working but Aunt Mae came. There were also a couple of dozen other people at least who you might have recognized but I did not know them by face.

It surprised me that your mother had no cemetery plot; that seems to me like the type of thing she would have taken care of, knowing her. Jimmy bought her a plot with Ruthie's family out in St. John's Cemetery, which is in Brooklyn and which really isn't far to go. The headstone isn't carved yet.

Connie put on a lunch for everyone back at their house. I felt like I had to go to it but I did not stay long. Most of the people did not know me anyhow and I wanted just to go home and be by myself. On the subway I felt like your mother was right there with me, that she did not have any more interest in it anymore either—the hubbub etc. Really, I think, in being alive. I hope you take this the right way, not that she was glad to go but I think she was. Enough is enough, I could almost imagine her saying. But she was only 41, so I do not know why I think that if I'm right.

It was not my intention to write all this but your Uncle Jimmy told me you would be glad to have the details of the last few days. That isn't what I thought but he understands more sides about you than me, having known you longer.

Spending time with her the past year and especially the last six months your mother seemed to get more lighthearted—honestly? prettier—and in the same time more older, "wisdom of the ages" and quiet. (Not that I think she was a big talker ever. Was she?) I'm still thinking about this, and I'll write more if I get it worked out.

That is about it. Jimmy and Connie want me to come to dinner at their house Saturday. Jimmy says there are things to talk about. I know there are—the lease on the apartment, clothing, furniture, etc. etc.

More tomorrow, baby. And the next day and the next day and the next day and all the days after that.

Among the worst things is a bad goodbye.

In May 1945 the war in Europe ended. Come summer Tallack was still in Britain. He expected to be sent to Japan, they all did. He was not pleased about it but he was resigned to the idea. On the 16th of July Marie penned a note.

"Can't wait for you to get here," she wrote, "so life can get started." A nice sentiment but not completely true, not for either of them. It was a—what's the word? It was a commonplace.

The British, meanwhile, were looking to get the nonessentials off their payroll fast. Only a month after the shooting stopped Syd Ballard was sent home. One day Cynthia and Tallack showed up for a milk run up to Derby and Syd's name was not on the manifest. Syd and Tallack were never close but he was a decent guy. Tallack would have been glad to see him off at least.

Tallack suspected that after the night in the truck alone with Cynthia Syd sensed something had changed, and this might have made him feel excluded. If that was right then no wonder Syd did not do anything about letting them know when he was demobbed. In later years Tallack was sometimes curious to know how things turned out for Syd.

Cynthia was discharged in late July and was going home to her family in Manchester to wait for Bert's return. She heard he was in a camp in Italy and was trying to find transportation home. On the day she should have been on a train to Manchester she met Tallack at a tearoom in a town called Flixton. Tallack never forgot that name.

"You're out of uniform," Tallack said when she walked in. Cynthia was not funny about her height like some women. She had a relaxed way about her body, the way athletes have. She wore the same clothes she had on the day she entered the army in 1942, a blue wool skirt and a polka dot blouse. In memory Tallack could never see the color of the dots; he could never dream in color either, so there might be a connection. But the texture of that blouse from when he touched her shoulder was a memory that would always be in his fingertips. He thought it was rayon.

"This skirt hangs off me. I'm nothing but skin and bones."

Civilian clothes made Cynthia seem shorter. In fatigues she could have been called imposing. When she took off her summer hat and hung it on a peg she let fall her copper-colored hair, always the most tremendous distraction to Tallack.

"What time is your train tomorrow?" Tallack sounded like he was prepared to stay until it left, and sort of mopey about it.

"I'll go at midday. I'm dreading it." Cynthia had been saying this for weeks and Tallack was past trying to answer with anything encouraging. "Until Bert gets home the family will not let me have a moment's peace."

"What are you hearing?"

"I'm not hearing. I'm told when I'm told, apparently. A week, a month. I remind myself how much harder it must be on him."

"Four years in a camp. I can't picture it." Even at the end of his life it cost Tallack something to say anything even remotely sympathetic about Bert/Tommy.

The stout lady who ran the tearoom kept popping up at the table. She treated them like lovers, which they certainly looked like, talking.

"And there is the matter of a job for us both. I don't know where to start. My cousin Iris offered to try and get me on at the bicycle factory she works in at Nottingham."

"Bicycling is big now, I'm told."

"Her husband died two years ago. She told my dad she has space to spare until we find a place of our own."

There were few people in his life whom Tallack ever liked the way he liked Cynthia. Don't think he did not know how tough she would have been to live with; Bert/Tommy was going to have his hands full. But Tallack enjoyed the way she said whatever came into her brain. She would pull the roof down on her head just for the change it would make.

And so here we are.

"You'll write all the time?" she asked.

"Of course. All the time."

"You're a liar. The world doesn't want men and women to be friends, Charlie. The world puts us on different teams. Anything else is a plot from a different novel."

"Cynthia, what would you like? Next week or next month

Tommy comes home. To you."

"Bert."

"Sooner or later I go home. To Marie. But you'll abandon me first. Is that even a point worth making?"

"This tea is cold."

"They expect you to drink it right away."

"I'm sorry to be childish. I would only like the world to stop—is that such a lot to ask?"

"You feel what you feel. But stop being this way. Your face looks like a tree full of owls." Tallack was interested to notice himself becoming impatient with Cynthia.

"I don't know what 'tree full of owls' means."

"I'm not sure I do."

"Sometimes," Cynthia said, "I think about committing a minor crime if that's what it would take to buy time. When I came out of jail everyone would shun me and leave me alone. That is what I'd like." You see what I mean about pulling the roof down on her head.

"I'd write to you in jail."

"Thank you. That would keep my spirits up." Cynthia looked about the tearoom to no purpose. "Time is short," she said, a line from some movie.

It was Tallack who left first. There was his bus to catch back to the base in Holton. Outside on the curb—*kerb* they spelt it—the pair of them waited, looking up the road for the bus coming, saying nothing. Tallack recollected a beautiful warm sun, so it had to be late afternoon.

"Don't forget me, Charlie."

"Never."

Tallack gave her his hand to shake on it. So she kissed

him. Then the woman who owned the tearoom came hurrying out waving Cynthia's summer hat that she left up on the peg. The lady looked from one of them to the other, waiting to be thanked, pleased to be a supporting player in this romantic scene until she noticed Cynthia crying.

Naturally the bus was right on time, which in the circumstances was for the best.

Tallack used to be a great one for naps. Unhappy though he was he fell asleep on the bus ride back to Holten. He did not hear from Cynthia again until the end of August, after the atom bombs finished the war in Japan. She wrote to him on onion-skinned paper in lavender-colored ink—women's ink.

> *Sorry to have gone silent on you, Charlie. I had your letter at my sister's house, thank you very much. Bert came home two days ago, and that was all right; you said it would be. He means well and we've talked things over. He appears unchanged.*
>
> *You will notice the postmark on this letter is Notts. We've moved in with my cousin Iris and good to her word she found me a job in the office of Hera Bicycles. She is a dear and has made us welcome. We're camping with her until Bert finds something permanent.*
>
> *With the war ended I know you'll be going home soon; I do hope this letter finds you or else what shall I do? I'm going on with life but I've forgotten nothing of our time in the lorries—two years riding around and smoking, can you imagine that that is how we won the war? It feels like a secret I share only with you, only you. Important as it was, I'll tell no one. Hold me to it.*
>
> *Yours, always,*
> *C.*

Tallack took that letter home with him. Since he did not recall tossing it out it must still be around, maybe in all the stuff he moved from the old house when he moved in with his son Dennis at the end of his life.

Tallack hated thinking of Cynthia with the husband. Lying in his bunk he hated the thought of her in bed with him; it ripped him up. But even more Tallack hated to think of her doing the routine things of the day with him, buying eggs or bread or something like that.

Tallack was half preoccupied with exactly that idea—buying the bread—on his first day home in New York. He was lying in bed with Marie. She was telling him all about their money.

Complication gives life savor.

It was October 1945. For a short while they lived with Mr. Brochain and Edward in their Bronx apartment. Uncle Jimmy broke the lease on Mrs. Tallack's apartment on East End Avenue soon after she died; given what he could get for the place at that time the landlord jumped at it.

Tallack's first night home he and Marie were awake until very late doing the early work on the creation of their first child, Maureen. Early the next morning, too early for Tallack, Marie was propped up in bed talking about what she called "the future," a conversation Tallack preferred to save for later. He made a nice joke along those lines but Marie did not want to hear it.

Tallack was having a hard job paying attention to what Marie was telling him, switching between upsetting thoughts of Cynthia in bed with Tommy and the pleasure of being in bed with Marie. After two and a half years he forgot what being in bed with a woman was like. Honestly, he barely recalled getting married.

Marie, on the other hand, had been feeling more and more married all the time.

A few days after Mrs. Tallack's funeral Uncle Jimmy and Aunt Connie asked Marie to come around to their house for dinner. They were looking out for her, sure, but Jimmy also had some legal business to discuss.

It developed that two years before Jack Tallack died Jimmy talked him into buying a $4,500 life-insurance policy which when he died two years later paid out. "What did he die of?" Tallack asked Marie. "Did Jimmy say?" To Tallack this was a more interesting question than the $4,500. That is saying something right there.

"Some blood thing. Jimmy *mentioned* that he did not recollect. Anyway, Jack Tallack died and Jimmy got your mother to put most of the money in an annuity."

"I don't know what that is."

"You think I do? What I know is that on the day your mother died it was worth something over $12,000. Some of it Jimmy repaid himself for funeral expenses and some your mother wanted to give St. Rita's. We're left $11,000."

Tell the truth Tallack was a kind of angry when he heard. Had his mother used the money she might have had a different life, been less uneasy all the time. When he made exactly that remark to Marie, though, she did not take it up.

"You got that off her? I never thought she was uneasy. I've been thinking we should open a clothes store. We'd be good at it."

"Starting a business is a risk."

"Everything's a risk. Which would you rather—go back to work being a floorwalker?" There in the bed Tallack closed his eyes and thought about his old boss at Gimbal's. Mr. Maunder the guy's name was.

"No.'

"You'd never make any money at it."

"I know."

Marie got up, naked, wonderfully naked. Tallack had not ever noticed the two big freckles on either side of her spine. They were not in the least symmetrical in their relation. And she was hippier than when Tallack left not quite three years before. He liked the extra meat on her. It was more womanly.

From an envelope on her bureau Marie brought Tallack two photographs of a storefront she had found two weeks previous.

"What do you think of 'Guys & Gals' for the name?" Marie asked crawling back into bed. "The beauty part of it is we could expand our line and never have to change the name down the road."

In the beginning when she talked about the store Marie employed the expression "down the road" all the time. Marie's whole world was down the road.

"The landlord said he would hold the lease for me to the end of the month on my promise to ask you. Because I told him you're a veteran. All you have to say is yes."

"Nice of people to die and leave us all this money."

"Don't look a gift horse in the eye. And that is really the thing."

"What's really the thing?"

"Your uncle told me something when he explained to me about the money. He wanted me to write it in a letter to you but I thought you should hear it from me in the flesh in case you get upset."

"You make it sound like something awful is coming."

"Nothing awful. A surprise."

"I like surprises."

"Something came up when I asked after your Aunt Ruthie at dinner with Jimmy and Connie."

"Ruthie's my cousin."

"She is not."

"I think I'd know, Marie."

"She was your mother's sister-in-law."

"Mother did not have a sister-in-law. There was nobody on the Tallack side we had anything to do with."

"But Ruthie's name was not Tallack. It was Dempster."

"I'm sure there was an explanation."

"That she is your aunt."

"What are you talking about?"

"I always suspected something in your family, Charles." Marie sounded like a detective from the movies. "Jimmy," she told Tallack, "came around your mother's one time to visit when I was there. Ruthie was along with him and he was handing out advice to everybody the whole time like he does but chiefly to Ruthie, like she was his ward or something."

"'Ward' is a good word for Ruthie."

"She was feeling down. It was right after when Ruthie broke her engagement."

"Ruthie was never engaged. There's never been any man in Ruthie's life. That is among her characteristics. She is a ward."

"You wouldn't know this. If you had been here they would have been telling you about it. The whole thing didn't last a year."

"You aren't kidding?"

"I never met the guy but your mother did. He was from Ruthie's church. Your mother said he was younger than her and that he had some, I don't know what, *ailment*. Ruthie went head over heels, you know?, the way middle-aged people do who've never been in a romance."

"You know that how?"

"Observation. According to your mother, Ruthie looked again at this fella and concluded life at home was not so bad. I remember your mother saying, 'Marriage is no cure for solitude.' From what your mother said Ruthie was pretty broken up."

"I don't picture a man ever wanting Ruthie."

"That's mean."

"It is not, honest it's not. The idea is beyond me."

"That's only because she is your aunt."

"Cousin."

"You're being a nuisance, Charles. I'm trying to work around to a point and you're causing me to beat on the bush."

"Now what?" Tallack said. Marie was packing too much into his first morning home. For at least a while Tallack wanted to be a blank.

"That your last name should have been Dempster," she said, "*not* Tallack. *That is* what. Really, legally, I don't know. But it is Dempster."

"What the hell are you talking about?"

"Your uncle told me. Get that man going and he's quite a chatterbox. The story is that Dempster was your mother's first boyfriend when she was about 19 and got her pregnant."

"Go on."

"You *know* go on, Charles. She was pregnant with you.

They got married before you were born, but then he died."

"Dempster."

"Dempster died, exactly. That was when your mother met Jack Tallack. But then Tallack died too. See?"

"I do not believe it."

"Something, isn't it?"

"Poor mother. First this guy Dempster. Then Jack Tallack."

"At the start of it all poor mother, but Jimmy said once she got started your mother was happy just you and her. Are you upset?'

"I'm taking it in."

"Amazing she didn't ever tell you."

"She might have meant to. I got the signal I was not supposed to talk about anything that happened to her before I came along. Like about that picture my mother had of him on her bureau."

"Of Tallack?"

"I always thought it was Tallack. Now I don't know. I don't even know what job he had."

"Dempster?"

"Tallack. Or Dempster. Christ."

"Your uncle said Dempster worked making pianos. Does that give you anything to go on?"

Women are the origin of everything.

Without the shove from his wife Tallack never would have been his own boss. By the time he got out of the service Marie had already made contact with suppliers in addition to scouting the storefront. The space was in a building owned by a fellow named Reuben Tenuta, who was kind of an operator but not at all a bad guy.

On the Saturday after Thanksgiving, 1945, fourteen weeks after Tallack came home, Guys & Gals opened for business.

Tallack and Marie were 22 years old.

Tallack's granddaughter Abbie once asked him what his strongest memory was. He gave the question serious consideration. Babies kept coming up in his recollection.

Once, for example, when Marie was pregnant with Maureen, Tallack had a big dream that he always recalled so well that it was as if he had had it only the night before. That was the first time he had been around a pregnant woman so much, and naturally he was in awe of the whole business. Tallack could not get over Marie's ballooning belly, a baby in there. In the last months of the pregnancy he liked lying next to her in the bed at night, fascinated. Hand cupped over her stomach and feeling the baby kick. This particular night the way she frisked around Maureen seemed to jump like a jitterbug. Tallack went off to sleep dreaming of the baby stretching and stretching and stretching Marie's stomach, stretching until the skin was so taught he could plainly see the eyes and nose and baby ears and a great round moon face.

"You are beautiful," Tallack said to the moon face. That was all the dream.

If anyone really wanted to know Tallack's big memories it would have surprised them to hear that among them was a cool bath on a summer afternoon.

It was 1953. It must have been a Saturday, the day Tallack always closed the shop at three. He came home hot and sticky, and maybe a little cross because of that. All he could think about was a bath. This was before Johnny was born.

Out in the backyard Maureen and Dennis were running through the lawn sprinkler. In the tub, up to his neck in the water and smoking a cigarette, Tallack heard them laughing. Even with eyes closed Tallack could find the ashtray on the bathroom floor. He enjoyed smoking in the bath. To him this felt like luxury.

Marie came in and sat on the lid of the toilet for a chat. Between her fingers was an unlit cigarette.

"Got a match, buddy?" she asked him. Wet and naked Tallack pretended to search his pockets.

"That's OK. I shouldn't smoke. How's the water?"

"Come on in."

"How'd the day go?"

"Long."

"Make money?"

Tallack nodded, still with eyes closed.

"Some days I wonder if I can spend the rest of my life like this, selling clothes to parents whose kids would rather be anywhere than in the store. I get tired of jollying the little bastards. I could smack them half the time, they're so fresh."

He took a deep drag on his cigarette before stubbing it out in the ashtray beside the tub.

"But yeah, we made some money."

They always made money in August. Guys & Gals was one of two stores in Ilkeston that sold uniforms for St. Martin's School. Every August the little Catholics who attended the school came to the store to get measured for uniforms. They came until they were 13 years old, right through the years when all kids do is grow. It was wonderful the way they needed new uniforms each year. A boon from nature.

"Think we'll have anything for the savings this month?"

"No. July was an expensive month, and we never do much business. August we get even. September, I think." Marie knew the answer before Tallack spoke. She was the one who kept the books, the money-minded one between the two of them.

"We've got to get more religious about putting money aside," she told Tallack. "That is the way to wealth, they say."

This looked like one of those conversations when Marie felt the need to talk about finance; Tallack imagined slipping under the water until she went away. If ever he had to think about money Tallack got depressed, even in those periods that found them in the black; Tallack never trusted solvency. By the time Marie was dead it was not on his list of concerns anymore.

"I don't think wealth is really on the cards for us, Marie." Out in the back yard Maureen yelled like an Indian fighter—murderous—chasing her little brother Dennis through the sprinkler.

"Do you think we'll ever get to the point where we've paid off all our debts?"

"Not unless we put the kids out to work," Tallack told her. "But there's enough."

"If we have another there's not." Marie hid her eyes from him. She bent her head so that her red hair fell across her face, veiling her.

"Another what?"

Marie was crying. Which worried Tallack because they had obviously been doing all they could to cause it to happen. In the filmy bathwater he knelt and took Marie's shoulders in his hands.

"Why are you crying? This is good news."

"You're all wet."

When she was only 31 Marie had a ruptured uterine cyst. There was an infection and their doctor, Dr. Nichols, recommended a hysterectomy. After the surgery Tallack was relieved to find none of it changed anything about her desire. Sex should be conversation, and Marie liked conversation; to the end of her life she had an urban personality.

Marie had the better touch for retailing than Tallack and she always would. She had the strength of her sociability. She liked the mixing, liked the gossip with customers, liked the small talk and the flirting salesmen—the daily stuff of it. Marie had the feel for business as good sport. Winning was best but nothing was personal. She had instincts Tallack did not have for wrangling credit extensions from suppliers, say, or dickering with Reuben Tenutta when he came around every two years to raise the rent.

Each time it was the same thing. Marie and Tallack leaning with arms folded against the wall behind the display case, waiting to hear what Reuben would offer. Reuben leaning on the case with a notebook open, thin guy with a gray crew cut, smiling. He began by addressing himself to Tallack, man to man, you know, and explain how he needed to raise the rent.

"Everything's gone up this year," Reuben would say. "All my expenses." Then he named an amount.

"Reuben!" Marie would cry, shocked by his cupidity (greed). But she was laughing so Reuben laughed too.

"It is the best I can offer, Mrs. Tallack. I'm in business too. There's been a lot of inflation."

Then the bargaining began. However long the term of the lease Marie wanted six months more. Or a promise to point up the bricks out front. Or both. She pressured Reuben to harass the couple in the adjacent shop, the Heilmans. Theoretically the Heilmans ran a newsstand but in fact they took bets. Their shop was barely lit and the weeklies in the racks out front were yellowed with age.

Marie's shrewdest maneuver was hiring Reuben's brother. Rolfe had no experience but he had a history.

Before the war Rolfe was a good club boxer. Around town he was known for spending his purses on fancy threads; this could be interpreted as a retail-clothing connection. Rolfe was captured in the Ardennes Forest at the Battle of the Bulge and spent that last winter of the war in an unheated Belgian barn before the Germans moved him east. By the time he was liberated Rolfe was not nuts but he was certainly changed. And no good as a boxer anymore; too shaky. Instead he earned a kind of living caddying at the Ilkeston Golf Course. And his brother Reuben paid his rent.

One of their prosperous years, a year Marie and Tallack actually needed help, Marie asked Reuben if he thought Rolfe might be interested in a job.

Rolfe turned out to be a good worker. The kids who came in liked it when he pretended to spar with them. Rolfe had a simple man's focused mind, which made him good at stockkeeping. And for four years Reuben renewed the lease without an increase.

The Tallacks made a good living from that business. Two or three years they made lots of money, so much it frightened Tallack, genuinely; people like him never expect money and do not always know what to make of it when it comes. But Guys & Gals was never Marie's idea of the big leagues, let's face it, though they owned it forty six years.

In those years when she did not work in the shop full time Marie was lonely. In daylight, with husbands away at work, women ruled their street. All her life Marie never liked the company of women unmixed with men. It did not have spice enough for her. Marie liked her life with spice.

The only woman in the neighborhood with whom Marie ever felt an inclination to be friendly was the mother in the house across the street, Delores Tresca. Delores was married to Alen Tresca, a professor at the local campus of the state university. Alen taught economics. Short and plump(ish) and pretty Delores was considered a character by everyone—including Marie, who liked her. Tallack believed Delores cultivated eccentricity. That way she kept her distance from the other women in the neighborhood. In Marie's eyes that might have made her an ally.

Delores kept her hair long and braided, even into old age when it went all yellow white.

Once when the kids were still young but in school Marie went missing. It was 1961. The children came in one afternoon and their mother was not in the house. They waited and waited until Tallack came home; Maureen capitalized on the opportunity for being in charge and bossed her brothers around while they waited for Tallack to come in.

Tallack heard their story and then made up one of his own. He cooked their dinner and put them in bed. At last about ten o'clock he heard the car pull in the driveway.

"*Where* have you been?" Tallack was angry. He was seldom ever angry.

"I had shopping to do."

"Where?"

"At the Orbach's." This was a plausible answer. Around

that time the first big mall had opened near them and Marie worried that it might draw customers away from small independent shops like theirs.

"Shopping the competition?"

"After a fashion." The pun was unintended. Marie did not make puns.

"You didn't buy anything?"

"That is not why I went."

"I hate when you won't give me a straight answer."

"To see it, Charles. Nothing more complicated than that. Just to see it. Forgive me losing track of the clock."

"That was unlike you."

"Then I apologize."

Later in bed she was silent, which sooner or later always made Tallack feel like he was the one who needed to apologize. Married people know the effect they have on one another, and exploit this where they can. This is an aspect of living intimately.

"Tell me more about going to Orbach's." You see, Tallack showed interest.

"I had to go in for the old time's sake." Marie spoke from beside him in the dark, the scent of her day's last cigarette still on her breath. "It is much more glamorous now. The displays are *chic*, you know? They use a much better class of mannequin than we could ever afford. They spent money on everything, and it gives you a nice feeling to walk around. And there I was among the dowdy ladies. Another dowdy lady admiring the pretty clothes."

"You're not dowdy."

"Don't bother, Charles. They had mirrors everywhere."

Unable to check her retailer's instinct she added, "I wouldn't do that. Put up all those mirrors and it leaves no illusions. It doesn't make a woman want to buy. It makes her want to hide."

There is no shame in private doubts.

The longer we live the more we have a need to picture ourselves outside the incoherent web of choices we have made. We will dream of some second life, one in which we are not having to think about money every twenty minutes.

It might be said that Tallack had Cynthia Hipsley for that second life. As far as ever he knew until much later Marie had no one.

Until he died Tallack averaged about two or three letters a year from Cynthia. Usually they were several pages long and felt written more for herself than for him, which was fine, he was glad to read them anyway.

Always there was one around Christmastime and then at least one other that when it came felt unexpected.

At first Tallack was funny about the letters. He told Marie they were from a British army buddy, letting her assume the buddy was a man. After a while Tallack suspected

Marie knew no man used the pretty colored inks—*mauve* and so on—Cynthia liked. At some point Marie started saying "Letter from home" whenever an airmail envelope with a Notts postmark showed up. Ignoring a lot is an important trick of being married. That sounds like a joke but is not meant to be funny.

For Cynthia one life would not have been enough, which is an admiring thing to say about someone. In spite of herself she was married to Bert/Tommy long enough to have a son and bring the boy up—longer than that, as a matter of fact, because if Tallack recalled correctly the son was away in college when the marriage ended. Once the son was off on his own Cynthia went to college herself. Even at the time she described it as

> *...a new leaf on life. I am among boys and girls, babies, most of them not half my age. They treat me like a sage, Charlie, even the professors, because I am so <u>old</u> at 43. When I'm not being annoyed it is funny.*
>
> *At times I think of Bert, strangely enough, even now. Looking rearward I see him now as the 'friend of my youth,' my old pal. We both found that insufficient, and one day it seemed as if we simultaneously looked across the dinner table and said to ourselves about the other one, "They must be gotten rid of." Amazing how well we understood each other in certain ways. Ah well, life advances. Naturally we're in touch; after all, we share a child and that is something. Bert teases me good naturedly about going to college. To repeat, when I'm not being annoyed it is funny.*
>
> *I have met a boy at the college. Odd writing that; it*

> *sounds jejune. We share the same tutor and cross paths (funny, I nearly wrote "cross swords" just then) cross paths every Thursday morning. This has led to regular coffees. He is 29—like me he's classed as an "older" student but still from a far different world than ours, Charlie. On my side it is only play. I will not allow him to become too smitten (!, as I've known you to write). (I hesitate to tell you all this—<u>should</u> I hesitate, Charlie?)*

Be this as it might.

Tallack was glad to hear Cynthia's stories whenever she wrote. She was interested in herself, and up to a point that is appealing. In time she married "the boy"—Ian or Ewan or some name like that, but in Tallack's memory it seems he came and went, whatever his name may have been. He strayed—Tallack recalls Cynthia using that word—*strayed*, an old-fashioned way of saying it, as if she needed to make a joke of what happened. Tallack did not recall her ever mentioning him again, but it was all a long time ago, buried under an avalanche of so many other things he was expected to recall.

Finally there was Jack. Or David. Tallack never remembered. That marriage went the distance, or at least until Jack/David died. Everyone was in their seventies then. Cynthia's son eventually had a wife too but something happened to her.

Tallack had no proof but he believed women are better made than men for the long pull. Which is to say, for when something happens.

We thrive on illusion and misdirection.

In those days Ilkeston was a suburban town of about 11,000 people. Some were new families like the Tallacks but others were people who had a connection to the town that went back a hundred years. Later it built up and the feeling of an old place was erased, though it took another 20 years after the Tallacks arrived for that to happen. It was a segregated place. At that time no one gave this much reflection.

It was 1958. The Tallacks' shop was in a row of four-story buildings put up in the 1890s. These looked like part of a movie set for pictures set in the imaginary America, and it was.

The picture was called *Against All Currents*, which before it was a film was a famous novel. Tallack could never explain the title though he appeared in the movie as an actor and afterward read the book, which he finished.

The way this came about was that Marie and he were paid $2,400 to close the shop for three days so that the movie producers could film on the sidewalk in front of Guys & Gals. They also asked to remove the Guys & Gals sign and replace it with one made for the movie. Tallack said to Marie he had no interest. She explained that he was an idiot if he said no, because of the publicity. (Helen Darrow, a big star at that time, was already cast in the movie.) And when did they ever do $2,400 in three days? (In the end there was an article about making the movie in *The Ilkeston Record* and that was all there was in the way of publicity.)

The moviemakers, Tallack believed, picked up on his reluctance and that was why they asked him to do what they called a "walk through," hoping to make him more agreeable. For this they would pay Tallack $600 for a morning's work. He had already taken their $2,400 but he said all right. Now he and Marie were up to $3,000 even.

On a Sunday afternoon in late June trucks and electricians and so on filled up the street in front of Guys & Gals. The Tallack's three kids watched it all and enjoyed the commotion. The first thing the movie crew went to work on was the sign. Seeing that sign come down felt like bad luck to Tallack, though it was not.

They wanted Tallack at 5:30 the next morning for his walkthrough. He was to wear his best suit if he owned one. He woke up that day with a heavy summer cold. By midday he would have a temperature of 102.

Day was breaking when he got there. Overnight the movie people had made over everything. Three big cameras were set up, bigger than Tallack would have imagined. Because a fancy grocery was the business run by the heroine in *Against All Currents* the window of Guys & Gals was filled with cans of food and cured hams (which were made of wood and painted). Above the door an awning said "Milton & Daughter" in pink and white.

Tallack asked a technician why the hams were red and the stripes were pink.

"Pink reads red," the technician explained. "Red nobody uses it. But red you still want to see. It needs to pop."

There could have been 200 people in the street watching the filming and hoping for a glimpse of Helen Darrow. Someone brought her over to Tallack and they shook hands. She had a good face under all her makeup—a real face, broad. To Tallack's eyes her face was better than it was when she started in movies. It was a more impressive face than what is ordinarily called beautiful. Now they are all so gaunt.

For the scene he was in Darrow had to be up a ladder cleaning the front window with a cloth. Mrs. Milton (Darrow) climbed the ladder barefoot and someone handed up her shoes. She waved to everyone with a cloth she was holding and the crowd cheered. Seeing a movie star made them happy.

Tallack's walkthrough would be seen at the very beginning of the movie, the first scene. It was supposed to be morning. Walking past Tallack was to call out "Good day!" to Helen Darrow up on the ladder. That was all he had to do. Who he was and what he was doing in the movie did not matter. The idea was that this man he was pretending to be was strolling along and when he looked up he was struck stupid by the sight of Helen Darrow's backside, just like the men out in the audience would be. The director of the movie, Robert Engle, told

Tallack this was called an establishing shot.

"Movies are called 'pictures' for a reason," Engle said. "And you never go wrong opening on a laugh."

Tallack was smart enough not to try "acting." Engle wanted him to leer when he walked under Helen Darrow on that ladder, but outside of the movies and so on not many men really leer like that. And when they do they looked to Tallack pathetic, not funny. So he ignored Engle's direction. He tucked his glasses in the breast pocket of his suit jacket (from the vanity) and walked through, calling up "Good day!" to Helen Darrow.

Engle hurried over and gave Tallack a hug; the movie people seemed to hug a lot. This was not to Tallack's taste. Engle said he could see the "resistance" in Tallack's face, and he liked the effect.

"It shows you're trying not to look at her ass," he explained. A thing about Engle that Tallack always remembered, he never sat down. "Do it again for me," he said. "Wouldja?"

They kept the second one; Engle called him "two-take Tallack." The only problem they had with Tallack was that when the sound was played back he could not be heard so well. While Engle set up the next shot they had Tallack up on the roof of the building with a sound engineer, Tallack shouting "Good day!" in the open air over and over, loud as he could. Tallack was never comfortable up on roofs, for reasons no one needs to explain.

Eventually they got what they wanted. And that was expected to be the end of Tallack's movie career. He went home and went to bed with his fever.

Among the many things Tallack never thought about was that movies leave out all of what, in living, is most of how we spend our time. But who would pay money to watch a story that was supposed to cover six weeks that took six weeks to watch instead of two hours? No one.

One other thing Tallack never thought about was that even after writing a script people notice things in a story that do not make sense. That is what happened in *Against All Currents*.

The reason *Against All Currents* caused a scandal when it came out was that Lorraine Milton, the character played by Helen Darrow, becomes pregnant by the handsome science teacher at the local high school. If people in the little town they live in find out everybody's lives will be ruined. In the book Mrs. Milton takes the train to New York for an abortion. Naturally she is upset enough already but then the woman who arranged the abortion soon has troubles of her own and tries to blackmail Mrs. Milton for money. Very steamy for the time.

The difficulty for the movie was that no one could speak the word "abortion." Robert Engle dreamed up a scene that was not in the book in which Mrs. Milton takes her reputation in her hands and goes to see the kindly judge who lives in the town. To this judge she tells everything about the dreamboat science teacher and her difficult life and the getting pregnant. She tells the judge she "lost" the baby. There was no such scene in the book and there was no such judge. So Engle promoted Tallack from passerby to judge and called him back for more filming.

The actual Tallack was only 35, too young for anyone to believe Mrs. Milton would come to him for sage advice. To age him up they dusted Tallack's hair and eyebrows. Engle told him all he had to do was appear to listen while Helen Darrow explained what was happening in the movie so far. For this they paid $1,200 because Tallack had lines to speak. He said things like "I see" and "Have you told Marion?"

Now the Tallacks were up $4,200.

The scene in the judge's office was one day's work. They filmed it on a soundstage in Astoria, Queens. Like a glamorous movie star Tallack took the commuter train there. For him it was all fun and money; for Engle it was business.

Another day Tallack spent hours in a variety of suit jackets doing "reaction shots" that Engle could have on the shelf if he needed them later. He would say to Tallack, "Charlie, give me concern." That was easy; Tallack just pursed his lips. "Show me your acquaintance with human weakness," which cracked Tallack up. He stared off to the left and studied a fuse box for as long as he could without laughing.

"Give me equanimity," Engle said. Blank stare.

Then there was a Sunday morning when Tallack spent three hours going up and down the steps of the Ilkeston library, which stood in for a courthouse. Engle wanted these shots to "establish" Tallack being whatever kind of judge he was.

At the film studio in Los Angeles they watched Tallack's little bits in the movie and thought they made sense. Not Tallack they liked but the judge who said, "Good day!" and "Have you told Marion?" From that point on whenever

Engle woke up to a hole in his story they would dream up a little scene in which Mrs. Milton went to see the judge and explained everything. Tallack's part was to ask the questions the audience was probably asking itself. "Are you feeling better now?" or "When will Marion be home?" The judge apparently had so little to do with his time that he was always free whenever Mrs. Milton came by to talk about her problems.

That summer Tallack was paid $7,200 just to make himself available. That made $11,400 altogether. To that point Marie and he never cleared so much in a full year. They saved every penny of the movie money.

Until they wrote the credits that roll at the end of a movie it did not occur to anyone to give Tallack's judge a name. Engle thought about it and decided Tallack would be Judge Daylong.

Tallack asked him, "How did you come up with that?"

"Because, Charlie, a judge is honest as the day is et cetera—get it?"

Helen Darrow was not actually present for a lot of the scenes Tallack was in. Engle just cut and spliced to make it appear that she was. But Tallack got to know Helen a little, and she was friendly. To that point he only knew her from being on the *Tonight Show*, where she was always joking with Jack Parr about visits to her psychiatrist. She seemed sane to Tallack.

She gave him acting tips. His favorite was, "Don't think about what you're doing, Charlie. Your audience will fill it in for themselves." This is true for more than acting in motion pictures. Just ask the people who read about Tallack's father in the newspaper after he jumped from the roof. To them the whole thing—the whole sequence of events—had a logic, if they could only know it.

Tallack's last day as an actor Engle sent them all home about 11 in the morning. He had spent two hours that morning repeating "Will you promise to say this to Tara?" while Helen stood behind him looking out at the "rain." Engle was trying out different ways he could light her face.

It was a soft late-summer morning and for something to do Helen offered to drive Tallack home to Ilkeston. He was never so relaxed around her that he did not find it unexpected to be riding in a movie star's car with the movie star at the wheel.

Helen had been a name people recognized for 15 years or more. She was in her mid-thirties then, like Tallack, and for a woman in the movies that is getting to be old. As Mrs. Milton she was playing the mother of a teenage daughter.

"Bob Engel told me he wants to use you again," Helen said.

"He spoke to me about it."

"Why don't you do it?"

"I'm not an actor. You are an actor. For me the novelty's worn off. Plus I look in the mirror and I observe that I'm not Gregory Peck."

"You will more than do."

"He wants me to pretend I'm a judge again."

"You've definitely got a face for it."

"I haven't got the bug you actors do, Helen. I spent too much time listening to the stories you were all telling between setups about being broke all the time and wondering if you'll ever work again. Not you but even Tal Diamon." Tal (real name Dominic Tropiano) played the science teacher in *Against All Currents*. Years later he killed himself when his looks went and the roles dried up.

"Actors love the life," Helen said. "They all live in hope that lightning will strike and they'll be in a hit."

"It holds no interest for me." There was an edge on Tallack's voice that surprised him. Most of the time he was never the edgy type.

Big cars are quiet and the quiet in Helen's car filled it up. Tallack did not know why they had got talking about these things, why they did not stick to the small talk. He pushed his glasses up snug on the bridge of his nose.

Tallack said, "There was an actress who lived in our building when I was growing up. My mother was always after me to keep an eye out for her because the woman was pretty old and to get up to her place she had to climb stairs. Little by little, you know, she told me her life story. Turned out she had been in silent movies and Broadway shows I'd never heard of. When all that ended the woman had nothing. I recall people from the relief board coming to see her. Checking to see if she wasn't secretly sitting on a stash of cash and jewels, I suppose. Sometimes I carried things up the stairs for her, and there was nothing in the apartment. All she had was a bed, not even a radio to pass the time. It was not the poverty that got me. It was her solitude, like you can't imagine."

"Christ, Charlie, you're scaring me."

"That will never happen to you."

"Loneliness frightens me. That and I think I'm claustrophobic. The two of them."

"You'll never be lonely. There's always a crowd around you."

"And that has got what to do with it?"

"You're talented."

"I believe in luck," said Helen. "Talent helps. I'm not modest. I like the fuss and I like the paychecks. But I'm lucky. It might easily have been some other pretty girl or some better actress who got my life. Sometimes I ask myself why it was not."

"What's your answer?"

"Haven't got one. I am not a philosophical person, Charlie. It gets me nowhere."

She shook out a cigarette from a pack she had behind the sun visor and offered Tallack one. Then she said, "A month ago I found out I'm pregnant. Keep that under your hat, please. I mean it, Charlie."

"Of course. That's terrific."

"Wouldn't the judge say something along the lines of 'Have you told Marion?'"

"And how are you now?"

"You know I'm not married?"

"I don't know anything about you."

"Well, Charlie, I'm not. And that makes life awkward. But I ended one pregnancy when I was 22. I won't do it again."

"Good for you. You'll like it, I'm sure you will."

"A baby? I'm *not* sure I will like it. But these last five months playing Mrs. Milton every line I was given I tried to speak from my experience of knowing what a real abortion is like, not the movie kind that happens and no one will say it happens. A woman like Mrs. Milton is not grief stricken, Charlie. But she has a crack in her heart. It heals but it's in there. The challenge was making that crack entertaining enough to spend two hours with her."

"I'm not sure what subject you want me to talk about," Tallack told her. That was the truth.

"I'm telling you what makes an actor, Charlie. It is like having a second life, really a second life, the one I was meant to be living. It sounds nutty. Believe me it isn't. When I work," Helen said, "I'm never afraid of loneliness or old age or anything. Without the work I don't know where I'd be."

From there the conversation went to Helen's expectations for the movie and what she would do next. "Depends, I guess, on the baby," she told Tallack.

Helen dropped him at the house. After that day they never spoke again.

When it was released the next year *Against All Currents* did all right with the public. Once in a while it came up on TV; sometimes Tallack was indifferent, at other times he was interested to watch it. Years later his granddaughter Eileen told him that watching the film had become a Christmas Eve tradition in Poland; Tallack could not imagine why. One year Cynthia Hipsley wrote to say she never missed it when British TV showed it, just for the parts Tallack was in.

"I like seeing you frozen in time, Charlie," she wrote. "Are you still exactly that handsome?"

In 1962 they started a television program based on *Against*

All Currents. The surprising thing—surprising from Tallack's point of view—was that the character of Judge Daylong was as big in that show as the character of Mrs. Milton. Every week the pair of them had some problem to solve for someone in the town. Once again Judge Daylong appeared to have no home and no place he needed to go during the day but his office at the courthouse, where he was always available to Mrs. Milton. The handsome old actor they got for the judge played the part like everyone's favorite grandpa.

The series ran five years.

"Give me equanimity, Charlie," Tallack could hear Engle saying.

To Tallack it was like a metaphysical surprise, that from identical materials his judge could be made into someone else by the same name, simply by saying so.

By the time the show went off the air in 1967 Tallack was forty three years old, the same age as his mother when she died of pneumonia. Even then part of him thought he might yet have the "second life" Helen Darrow spoke about—not as an actor (!, as Tallack would put it) but as a role, a role in which life was edited to its interesting parts, and different from the life he got.

Thinking about this second life made Tallack somewhat discontented. This thought would press itself on him whenever he felt Marie was being bossy, whenever he worried his kids were growing up all wrong, whenever he found himself thinking about money days on end instead of—instead of what?

Then with impressive speed Tallack was old, his kids were grown, his wife was dead and he had just enough money to last until the credits rolled, fade to black, the end.

You must lie alone
Without hope, without life
Poor flesh, sad bone.

Robert Graves, "The Kiss"

Trouble comes at any time.

Growing up in the Bronx Marie Brochain lived downstairs from an elderly couple, the Famigliettis. They were retired on Mr. Famiglietti's railroad pension and survived into their eighties, which was a very long time to live back then. All the kids in the neighborhood knew Mr. Famiglietti. In the afternoons when the weather was warm he used to sit on the steps of his apartment house. The kids loved to hang around him. The kids told stories and the old man listened. The kids *vied* for his ear.

One day a boy from the neighborhood told Mr. Famiglietti about a boomerang he saw in the window of a hobby shop on the Grand Concourse. Mr. Famiglietti, like most people, had only ever heard of boomerangs. He was curious to see one. Taking a bus, he went down to the hobby shop and had a look. Price: $1. Mr. Famiglietti took the money out of his pocket and bought a boomerang.

Somehow every child in the neighborhood knew about Mr. Famiglietti's boomerang before he was home—"Indian telegraph," they used to call it. Without telling his wife what he was doing Mr. Famiglietti led the kids up to the local high school. On the baseball diamond he took the boomerang out of its box. He followed the instructions, holding it just so between thumb and forefinger down near the end of one blade. Imitating as well as he could the cartoon aborigine on the cover of the box Mr. Famiglietti flung his boomerang. It soared, as advertised, spinning higher and higher over the Bronx outback, over the school building. Everyone waited for the magical return back to Mr. Famiglietti, right back into his hand. Waited and waited. The boomerang came down on the roof of the high school and was never heard of again.

Mr. Famiglietti, Marie recalled, looked more than sheepish. He had blown a dollar on nothing.

The old man went home followed by his disappointed entourage. They exchanged theories of how the boomerang might have malfunctioned. At the door of his building Mr. Famiglietti was confronted by his wife, who lit into him in vituperative Italian. The kids all knew she was shouting about the waste of a dollar. Marie never forgot how humiliated Mr. Famiglietti looked.

And all over money.

As a girl it seemed to Marie that what happened to Mr. Famiglietti—what happened after he lost that boomerang—was what old age was about: impotence and the denial of small pleasures, a life of scraping by. Most people did not retire then. They stopped working when they had to and then held on for the end as well as they could. This was not the Tallacks' fate, and thank God. Still, with three children they had a hard job saving money.

Then they had a piece of luck.

It was 1991. The landlord of the Guys & Gals building, Reuben Tenutta, dreamed up a big plan to knock down the two store fronts he owned, Guys & Gals and the Heilmanns' stationery next door. Tenutta's idea was to build a three-story "mini mall" in their place. He offered to buy out the lease for Guys & Gals, a lease the Tallacks only signed four months before. After some back and forth Reuben offered $15,000 for each unfulfilled year of the lease, pro-rated—almost $60,000 in all.

"You're screwy," Marie observed.

But Reuben believed the real-estate boom would go on forever. He was also mayor of Ilkeston Park by then. Tallack's idea was that Reuben thought by being the mayor he would be able to snag some urban-renewal money from Washington for the little retail district that everyone in Ilkeston called "the village."

The only money that ever came from Washington went to build a multi-story parking garage. It was supposed to handle the flood of shoppers coming to the rejuvenated "downtown." This never happened. If he had not died first Reuben would have lost his shirt on that mini-mall scheme.

Still, it surprised Tallack that Marie was more eager to take up Reuben's offer than he was.

"We've been at it 45 years, Charles," she said. "Where else do you think this goes?"

After liquidating their inventory and banking Reuben's check the Tallacks had more money than they ever had altogether at once. Plus they had Social Security and the house was paid for. They were fine.

Their son Dennis, who understood finances a lot better

than his parents, invested the cash. He did all right by them and put the money into bonds and Treasury bills when the whole world was chasing technology stocks. He knew his parents; the Tallacks had no interest in financial thrills. They remembered Mr. Famiglietti.

Marie was better at retirement than Tallack; too bad she was not given more of it. Tallack's lack of skill in this area made the adjustment harder for him. He was not one of these geezers who recreated himself in old age. He did not take up bicycle racing or sculpting. He gave of his time, of which he now had so much. He did not travel the way some do. Tallack found travelling not exactly dull but work. Eventually the experience always felt the same.

Marie had been more curious than Tallack to see new vistas; she liked vistas. Several times she traveled by herself to Austin to visit their daughter Maureen and her family. It was like an adventure, flying to the far side of the country by herself, out there with the cowboys. Tallack encouraged her to go. He never mentioned that left home by himself he felt like an old dog, bereft.

Tallack had two daughters-in-law, the first of which, Dennis' wife Diane, gave him headaches. The second, Johnny's wife Shelly, was agreeable to him.

When Johnny married Shelly the Tallacks had been assuming their youngest son was past the time when he would marry anybody. Not that Johnny did not show early interest in pretty girls. Once Tallack found him up a tree outside a neighbor's bathroom window watching the wife there,

Christine Barcelona, shampoo her hair. There was such a lot of hair on Christine's head. It was black then and she wore it loose down the middle of her back like a girl. Certainly no one else's mother on their street wore her hair in anything other than a convenient cut that would not have suggested anything to anyone. A husband, maybe, once in a blue moon. To a 15-year-old boy like Johnny Tallack all that hair must have suggested a passionate nature, whatever a 15-year-old imagines a passionate nature to be.

Tallack happened to be taking the trash cans out to the curb and looked across the yard to see his boy up in a tree, silhouetted in the Barcelonas' porch light. Coming across the darkness of the yards he went and pulled Johnny down by his ankle. Nearly broke his neck, and then all the way home Tallack whacked him on the head. That was something Tallack felt bad about later in life. Tallack never hit his son Dennis for any reason at all that he can recall. Certainly he never hit his daughter, Maureen.

It did not hurt Shelly's case, with Johnny or for that matter with Tallack, that she had long dark hair like Christine Barcelona; Tallack's son had the luck to marry his earliest female ideal.

A light heart will only get you so far. At age 35 Johnny did not seem completely grown up to his parents; he seemed to be awaiting some boffo revelation that would explain everything to him. As Herman Melville remarked in a different story, Johnny looked like a man who had never cringed and never had a creditor. He was Johnny and never became John.

Like Johnny, Shelly Siperstein taught in the Ilkeston High School. The first night Johnny brought her to the house Marie and Tallack were impressed by several things at once. For one, Shelly was four years older than their boyish boy. Two, she was Jewish and the Tallacks were not. Three, she was already divorced not once but twice. Her first husband was a man who was avid for her at 23 but two years later said he no longer got the concept of marriage; imagine that. The next guy got the concept well enough that he asked release from his vows to pursue another marriage with a woman he met on his commuter train.

A fourth thing the Tallacks noticed about Shelly was that she was two months pregnant.

"Sweet Jesus," Tallack said. Not because anyone was pregnant. It was because Tallack looked at Johnny and foresaw everything that was coming.

"They're only *telling* you," Marie said. She was reminding Tallack of the commandment to be always—always—irrationally in favor of your loved ones.

But Marie would be the hard case about Shelly, not Tallack.

At first Marie barely spoke to Shelly. In the months before the wedding she made no offer to help. "Oh, you don't need my help, dear," she would say, but Shelly did need help. Her own mother was dead and her father Jack, in Tallack's opinion a completely wonderful guy, was on this job no help. Tallack was never completely sure that Marie did not intend what she said about Shelly not needing help as some kind of a wisecrack, an allusion to the fact that since Shelly had been down the aisle twice before she ought to have the route down pretty well.

The birth of a granddaughter, Eileen, did a lot to break the ice. Before long everybody loved everybody.

Shelly was with them the day Marie got sick. It was 1993, a morning in late May. Summer was about to pop. Tallack and Marie were on the front steps of the Buttonwood Street house. Marie was just after saying, "I am in a rare mood, Charles." This was the day she started to die.

Life can be gorgeous in spite of itself.

The crabapple in their front yard snowed pink blossoms on the green grass. In a thunderstorm the night before a lot of blossoms came down. Until after daybreak there was terrific rain, thunderclaps loud enough to set off car alarms. Now the day smelled new, perfumed. In the washed air birds kicked up a racket, hard at work on their nests and baby making; no day off for them.

Marie had the newspaper in her hand. By her feet was a chipped china mug with a blue iris motif that once belonged to her Aunt Mae.

Tallack lit his first cigarette of the day and sipped his coffee. He put his face up to the sun.

"You shouldn't smoke those things," said Marie.

"What's in the news today, honey?" His hands braced against two loose bricks in the top step. He was intending to fix them.

"The usual mayhem." Marie spoke without quite looking up from accounts of the previous day's atrocities and stranglings. "Helen Darrow's in a television movie this week. You two should reunite. You'd get good ratings."

"What's the movie about?"

"The war. It doesn't say what she does in it."

Across the street Delores Tresca's old collie, Silas, was stretched out under the sun. The same as Tallack he enjoyed the warmth on his bones.

Next door at the Barcelona's house a young man got out of a small blue car. With an air of assumed authority he walked across the front lawn, walked like someone born to leadership, like he owned the place. He bounced up the Barcelona's front step and clanked loudly on their brass knocker. Waiting for someone to answer the door the young man looked over in the Tallack's direction. He seemed about to smile but then appeared to have a change of heart about it.

Buddy Barcelona opened the door in a black sweatshirt and pajama bottoms; Charles Tallack slept naked every night of his married life, creating awkwardness for his children only occasionally.

The young man on Buddy's steps said, "Are you Mr. Dione?" Tallack's hearing was already bad in those years but even he heard the kid from across the street.

"No, I'm not Mr. Dione. You've got the wrong house." Buddy hissed in that rising tone cicadas make on a hot day.

"Which house is Dione?"

"There is no Dione on this block. And keep your voice down. My wife is sleeping."

The younger guy looked struck by perplexity.

"What?" he said to Buddy. "What?" He had been prepared to be genial.

"Keep your voice down."

"Buddy," said the kid, who could not know that Buddy's name really was Buddy, "buddy, I'll talk loud as I want." To make his point he raised his voice more. "Who the ***fuck*** do you think ***you*** are to tell ***me*** the way to talk?"

Buddy made a show of calmly pulling his door closed behind him, defending his sleeping family from this intruder. In one hand he held the newspaper he must have been reading when the guy knocked. He rolled the paper stiff. While the kid was focused on the newspaper Buddy shoved the kid off the stoop. The other guy jumped up and yanked Buddy down. They clinched the way men do when neither really wants to fight.

"Fuck you!" the kid said, stuffing his shirt into his track bottoms. "Fuck you! Fuck you!"

Nobody won.

The dog Silas was so disturbed by all this that he got up from his sunny spot on the grass and moved to the shade of a maple. More evidence against human nature, that's what the dog was thinking.

This same afternoon Johnny came with Shelly and their daughter Eileen to celebrate Shelly's birthday.

They were in the driveway studying a crack in the blacktop, which Tallack was pretty certain was brand new. "It bows like a parenthesis," Tallack told them. The crack brought to mind Helen Darrow because Marie had mentioned her. It was no comment on Helen's posture. Helen was an actress and her posture was excellent.

"Lightning is my guess," Johnny suggested. He traced

with his finger the invisible path of the pipe buried under them. "Trying to get at the sewer line."

"Your father says he can patch it," Marie said.

Everyone looked at Tallack.

"Soon."

Marie turned her attention toward the house. "Eileen in the basement?"

"She's working on our boat," Tallack told her.

In defense against the high afternoon sun Marie shielded her eyes.

"Why don't we go around back and sit down?" she said. "I'd prefer a little shade."

Eileen was where he left her, playing with the wooden boat on the basement floor. If the spirit moved her Eileen had a four-year-old's capacity for intense concentration. In everything that happened afterward Tallack always hoped Eileen never forgot how her parents delighted in her.

Johnny used to think Eileen had an interest in mechanical things that indicated positive prospects for her future. The Christmas before Marie got sick all Eileen wanted from Santa was a pocketed apron like the one she saw the garage mechanic using. It unrolled like a magic carpet, revealing all the silver-handled wrenches arranged inside. Eileen took it everywhere.

Tallack and she brought their boat upstairs to show everyone the progress they had made.

"We cut the gunwales on it," Eileen said.

"Where did you get a big word like 'gunwales'?" her mother asked.

"Papa told me it."

"Well that is a good word to use." The sun prepared to set.

Marie had an awful headache. Johnny brought her aspirin and sat with her. Marie kept her head absolutely still; she looked like a woman in a trance.

Shelly was with Tallack watching chicken cook on the grill.

"Did you ever smoke cigarettes?" Tallack asked.

"No."

"You seem like someone who'd sometimes like a cigarette."

"Thank you."

Chicken fat dripped through the grill and caught fire. Owing to the sizzling Tallack could not catch everything Shelly said. She told Tallack something about the high school. Tallack was not following and Shelly sensed it.

"Mom's feeling the heat today," Shelly said.

"She wasn't made for warm days."

Tallack made a summertime meal of the chicken with green beans and cold roast potatoes. There was enough early lettuce from the back garden to give everyone a salad.

Tallack lit the candles on a cake Johnny baked. They sang happy birthday, for Eileen's sake.

Marie's head hurt so much that she excused herself from the table. Then they wrapped it up.

Hunger is what nature intends.

Marie tossed all night. Her breathing came out in a rasp, an animal noise. To give her room Tallack went and slept on the couch. Whether this counts for a memory or is just an aside, that was the last night they ever lay next to each other.

In the morning Marie woke soaked in perspiration and needing to know the time. Beside the bed they had a clock. Marie complained its face was a blur.

"It's nearly eleven." Tallack was sitting in a chair beside the bed with the newspaper, waiting for Marie to wake.

"I slept so much."

"Do you want me to phone Dr. Nichols? I can take you."

"He never has appointments. And anyway he'll tell me to rest. I'm already resting." It hurt her to speak.

The clock ticked like a metronome—click click, just like that, mechanical under the other noises of the morning. Traffic through the neighborhood, someone swinging a hammer a couple of streets away, boys playing basketball out on Buttonwood Street, click click.

"You ought to wind that."

"It's electric. How are you feeling, honey?"

"I'm experimenting with just how little effort I need to keep my eyes shut. I'm glad you're here, Charles." When she touched him her hand was damp.

Through the open window came the basketball noise from next door.

"Doesn't he have a job?"

"Who?"

"That big boy next door. Sonny."

Marie rolled over and tugged the bed sheet up around her chin. She arched her back. From somewhere deep inside she let go of a big sigh, less a deep exhalation than the little moan people make when they are glad to be in bed.

"What day is this?"

"Monday."

"I'm cold." Ordinarily Marie was like a man in the way she did not mind cold. The most frozen night of the year she went around the house in bare feet and the sleeves of her blouse rolled up. But this was a blistering day, hotter than the day before and no birdsong at all.

Tallack stood to pull the window shade down.

"I dreamed," Marie said. "A man was climbing into the bed. He was slipping under the blankets with me."

"He looked like your husband?"

"No. He was wearing one of those sweaters with the buttons. What do you call them?"

"Sweaters?"

"I could see this bedroom and I could see you. I could see

trees out the window. I knew they were real. No matter how hard I wanted I couldn't make my limbs move."

Marie rolled over on her back.

"I was calling you but you were sound asleep." When she laughed she covered her mouth with the back of her hand. She did not have her teeth in.

"When the children were babies," she told Tallack, "sometimes I thought you were faking sleep so you wouldn't have to get up and heat the bottle."

"That's not what I recall."

Even without her teeth in Marie had a good face. Her silky white hair was swept away from her eyes, eyes teary with sleepiness. Tallack could see the girl she had been.

Little nose, little mouth.

Hope is a torment causing physical pain.

Tallack's second daughter-in-law was Diane DiNardo. Diane was a pretty girl who "got her hooks into Dennis," which is what Marie never forgot to say, got her hooks into Dennis at college. Marie's opinion was that her boy did not know how to say no to a dogged woman. Marie pictured Dennis manacled to Diane, especially as the years went by and Diane got preoccupied with the struggle to have a child. Dennis and Diane tried all the medical paths to pregnancy. They made abortive stabs at adoption, but children never happened.

Diane was short, you know, and her bosomy figure was out of proportion to her height. Clothes never looked right on her. They hung wrong.

Dennis, Tallack knew, was disappointed but did not see childlessness as some tragedy. Over time—two decades—Diane warped herself such that babies could not be mentioned in her vicinity without someone worrying she had been injured.

Marie knew the toll this took on her sweet-natured son. That was why she said what she did about hooks.

Tallack told her, "Dennis makes his choices."

One evening in that summer, an evening when the air was so wet Tallack perspired sitting still, one evening Dennis and Diane dropped around.

Marie was in bad shape. The night before she did not sleep, and through the afternoon her head was spinning. Twice she was sick to her stomach, nauseous from vertigo. Being sick gave her some relief. Each time Tallack had to change the sheets and start another laundry.

When Dennis and Diane came in Marie was adrift under a light cover of sleep. She opened one eye.

"How's the weather, honey?" Tallack asked her.

"Clear." Marie lay on her side, regarding all of them with the one open eye. The sun behind the curtains was the orange of the day ending. This was life breathing out before breathing in again.

Dennis squatted beside his mother. Coming straight from work he was in a suit and tie. At the back of his head was the beginning of a bald spot and only a speckling of gray. But Dennis had his soft baby face, unlined in a way to make you think, Here is a man with no worries.

"Pop says you had a rough day."

"Never have I felt so rotten."

"Ma, I'm sorry."

Diane took the chair where Tallack usually sat. From the heat of the day her face and bare legs were blotched.

Diane put her hand sympathetically on the blanket

covering Marie. Marie flinched. She rolled over on her side to get a better squint.

Diane smiled. "I came to see how you are."

Marie took in Diane's figure.

"Men like a big chest," she said after a moment. "They go for that."

"Don't let the men in on our secrets," Diane replied without missing a beat. Credit for that, Tallack thought.

Through June and July Marie stayed the same and intermittently got worse. She floated out of touch, losing any firm sense of back or forth. That she knew this was happening was the awful thing.

"I'm on the moon, Charles," she said, "looking back at the world through a telescope. Everybody looks at me."

"They worry."

About August odd things were coming out of Marie's mouth. "Whittle, whittle" she would repeat, or "nylon divide," just bits of language come loose in her head. "The stuff of night." "Once the beans." "The cellar's wet."

Every two weeks Tallack took Marie to see a specialist, Dr. Chand. It was depressing being in a waiting room full of aged people like themselves, grey-haired couples with one of them broken.

But Tallack liked Chand. He gave the impression of a man perpetually fretting about his patients. He was old-fashioned in that way.

Chand scheduled an MRI of Marie's head.

By the end of summer Marie was unconscious 12 hours a day. Tallack's problem was that he never knew which 12 hours it would be.

Tallack assumed the routines of someone with a new baby in the house, worrying over Marie if she did not sleep and grabbing the chance to pick up the house a little when she did. Sometimes there were things they needed from the grocery store and no one around who could get them for him. If Marie was sleeping soundly Tallack took a chance and dashed out to the convenience store at the gasoline station three streets over. The whole while he was worried she might wake up, imagining the million terrible things that could happen if she got out of bed. Burning the house down was one example.

At other times Marie woke comparatively clearheaded. She might walk down the hall from the bedroom with a sleepy smile and say like her old self, "Hello, love." The change in her would be so dramatic that Tallack thought maybe it was a miracle cure.

Hope is a torment causing physical pain.

We wish for miracles.

On their wedding anniversary, August 17th, Marie happened to be feeling well. She got on a clean bathrobe and had a wash while Tallack made her a sandwich she did not want.

They sat out on the front step and ate while they watched the street, like the two old city people they were.

The sky began to cloud over. That is a description of the actual sky, not a way of talking about the state of Marie's mind. A cold front was arriving. The temperature dropped perceptibly from moment to moment. The sharp edge of a cloud shelf was visible, a cliff of cold air. Tallack and Marie sat and watched it come on.

The color of the sky was yellow.

"The sky moves," Marie said. She always had a taste for drama, the sort of person delighted by a violent electrical storm. "The day we bought our wedding rings the light was funny that way. I remember watching it from your mother's bedroom. I can taste the light."

Tallack did not like her talking about the past. Past and present were all mishmash wherever it was she went when her brains floated off. "She's lost her moorings" was the phrase in Tallack's head, picturing his wife as a sad zeppelin drifting away beyond the hills.

"How is your head now?" His theory was that focusing on the present was better exercise for her mind.

"My memory hurts," she said. "Dead people come and tell me things. My brother Edward. I'm looking for you or I know something has happened to one of the kids but I can't find them. Everything is bent. I see things I know aren't there."

Her sandwich slipped from her hand. She stared at its parts around her dirty feet, as if she were trying to make sense of them.

And just like that she was swoony. Tallack helped her back to bed.

In a few minutes she slept. All summer caring for her was like playing Chutes & Ladders.

Chand gave Marie's MRI a mixed review. He prescribed more doctors. He sent Marie up to the hospital for blood tests. After that he had her sit for a psychological evaluation that by the usual measures of lucidity she flunked.

The psychiatrist suggested Marie might have the beginnings of—the onset—the onset of dementia. She said this to Tallack in front of Marie, as if she were not present. After that Tallack refused to go back to the guy.

Home from the hospital that afternoon Tallack phoned Chand.

"It's good she sleeps," Chand said when he rang back.

"For now I'll believe you."

"Start worrying if she can't sleep. What is she saying those times she talks?"

"Nothing close to sense."

"Take notes. Maybe there's a pattern."

That night Marie was a long while going off, talking and talking about nothing. Tallack took notes and did not hear anything in any of it. She was like a parrot stringing together phrases and names and words, oblivious to meaning.

"Do that nice. Where did Edward go?"

"Tell the lady not to sell the same way down to here."

"Leave the road."

"Why are you painting the wall?"

"Whose dog is that?"

Tallack did not care what Chand said; he could not find a skeleton key to it. Until midnight he sat with Marie. "Why don't you try going off to sleep now, honey?" Eighty times Tallack told her that.

"I would," she said, "if you'd stop blathering, mister!"

So Tallack had to laugh.

Every night Tallack now slept on the pull-out couch in the living room.

Maureen telephoned up from Texas to speak with her mother.

"How are you feeling, ma? Pop says you're better today."

"What are you making for supper?"

"Just pasta. Pop says you've got him doing all the cooking now."

"He sleeps so much. It is like having a tiger."

"How's your head?"

"Better. How is the boy?"

"Oh, they're fine. Lou drove Thomas to his American Legion game today. I told him to make sure he keeps his hat on standing in the outfield. It is hot as blazes down here. The boys ask about you, especially Willie. He's right here."

Silence.

"Ma?"

"Yes?"

"Willie's got us nearly talked into a trip home around Labor Day instead of waiting until Christmastime. What would you think?"

"If your father arrives."

"He won't need much persuading."

"The days are short this year. It makes me bad."

"I wish you felt better, ma. I wish we lived closer so I could come and see you easier."

"When was that?"

"Labor Day."

"Let me speak to Pop."

"Pop's with you, ma. Would you like to talk with Willie? He's right here."

"Who's there?"

"Me—Willie. Hi, grandma."

"Who's there?"

"It's Willie, grandma. Don't you recognize my voice anymore? Can you hear me?"

"What's the rule for that?"

"I think we got a bad connection, grandma. I better get mom back."

"Who do you turn to for help with the school?"
"Ma?"
"Here it is."
"Ma, I love you. Can you hear me?"

Kindness is never wasted.

Toward the end of all this was a Friday morning, a hot one from the moment Tallack woke up. On his backstep he had a breakfast of coffee and a cigarette. The milk in the coffee was sour—really awful; it smelled like a dead animal. Then the kitchen telephone rang.

"Charlie?" It was Shelly's father, Mike Siperstein. "I was over to see the kids last night. Things are not so hot with Marie they said."

"She's really sick, Mike."

"I wish I'd known before now. Why don't I come over today? It would give you a break."

With Mike the Tallacks always got along, especially considering the bumpy start between the families. From the beginning Mike was the one who called the marriage of Shelly and Johnny "nothing but good news the whole way," Mike who was excited that Eileen was arriving ahead of schedule, Mike who was unwilling to see religion as a problem—one of the few people in the world of whom that could be said. When he went to God Mike's welcome was great, surely.

The big headache was Shelly's brother Rene. He hated

the idea of his sister marrying a Christian, even a nominal Christian like Johnny Tallack. For Rene it was no compensation at all that the wonderful Eileen was being raised a Jew. His anger at Shelly for marrying out was biblical, like the language he used to express himself.

"I can never bless this marriage," Rene told Mike. "It is anathema."

"So no one asked you," Mike replied. "Pay no attention to Rene," he said to the rest of them. "He's a nut on this subject."

Poor Mike spent his retirement years performing a shuttle diplomacy between his two children, trying to "bridge things up," which was the way he put it; he would have had better luck teaching cows to yodel. To his face Shelly told her brother to go to hell. But these things leave a mark.

Hard feeling between his children mattered extra to Mike because apart from them he had no one much to talk to. His wife Abigail was dead already 20 years. Outside the circle of his family he did not know many people; older men are often that way. Mike was younger than the Tallacks but already retired from the U.S. Postal Service. A few years after Abigail died Mike was knocked down by a delivery van and broke his hip. He recovered, but on the advice of his doctor and his union he took advantage of the chance to retire early on a full pension and a disability check.

"Dumbest thing I ever did," he often said. "Ever since I've been sitting on my backside. Live and lament." Mike tried golf but he missed his buddies at the post office. Now he was telling Tallack, "Take the morning off, Charlie. Go someplace."

Mike's boxy brown Camry pulled in the driveway. Tallack checked on Marie and saw she was awake.

"I've got a good surprise, Marie." The doorbell rang. "Don't go anyplace." Marie's eyes followed Tallack all the way to the front door.

Mike at the door was all smiles. Marie lit up at the sight of him.

"Look who came! Doesn't he look nice?" It was a funny thing to say, but Mike did look nice. Fit as ever, tanned from the golf and his gray hair swept back handsomely off his forehead; to Tallack Mike always looked a little like Stan Musial. That day he was dressed up, natty in a pink sports shirt and gray slacks. "Natty" was a good word for Mike.

"How are you today, Marie?" said Mike. By then she had drifted off.

Tallack spent his free morning doing good. In the two years since their retirement he and Marie were volunteers delivering meals to "shut-ins" for a program run by the Ilkeston Community Hospital. The program was managed by a woman he knew simply as Mrs. Gascogne. She and Marie were friendly and talked. Tallack was cordial.

At the hospital Tallack parked in back beside the dumpsters. In the heat that day the smell of food waste made a stink.

The kitchen was hot, busy, noisy. A television was forever switched on, always tuned to the same blonde woman reading the news. No one seemed to listen to this woman, although everyone glanced her way when they walked past; television demanded that.

The kitchen was lit in a flat fluorescent light that made people appear to be embalmed. Tallack recognized faces but no one knew his.

Mrs. Gascogne was elsewhere. From a warming table Tallack collected his trays. The route was taped to them on top.

Since the last time one of the regulars died. That was Mrs. Heilman, who ran the newsstand/betting parlor next to Guys & Gals. Those times when Tallack came by for the Home Visitors they never talked about old days, though Tallack was certain she recognized him. Another client, a blind man who lived in subsidized housing and liked to sing old songs, was arrested for allowing his apartment to become a "gambling den," in the purple prose of the *Ilkeston Weekly Record*. How could a blind man run a gambling den? He would need a good memory.

Another woman on the route was taken to an institution. She lived in a filthy barn behind her indifferent brother's house. Tallack thought she was better off out of there.

Last on the route was Mrs. Posner, who lived in the neighborhood everyone still called The Orchards because a farmer once grew peaches there. For a long time it was home to a colony of White Russians, who moved there in the 1920s after a Romanov prince who made a lot of money in Argentina (no one asked how) bought the property and built a church, onion tower and all. Mrs. Posner came to America well after all that and married another émigré, a man from St. Petersburg who Americanized his given name to "Derwent." Tallack always wondered where he got that. Derwent was a music and math teacher at the Ilkeston High

School, and in fact taught the clarinet to Tallack's daughter Maureen.

On her kitchen table Mrs. Posner kept a photograph showing Derwent in a wintry scene—homburg, overcoat with a fur collar, bare trees, grays and charcoals. He leaned against the grillwork of his car, smiling and as if saying, "This is a good kind of car to own."

Mike Siperstein's visit was doing Marie good. She was in her cotton robe, bare legs sickly white but for the gray soles of her dirty feet. She was crooning.

"What do you think, Charlie?" Mike said when Tallack came in. "Right from the time you left your wife has been singing like a bird. I could not keep her in bed."

Marie laughed behind her hand. The joke was on her.

"We've had a hundred renditions of 'The White Cliffs of Dover.' I haven't heard that one in years." Between them Marie and Mike had a pitcher of iced tea on the coffee table. Mike fixed it.

"There'll be bluebeards over the white cliffs of Dover." Marie warbled in a little voice. "I thought he was the fireman."

"The fireman?"

Mike glanced at Marie and she laughed more. They were conspirators.

"So?" Marie said to Tallack.

"So what?"

"So? So where were you?" She sounded a little irritated.

"I did the Home Visitors. I told you before I left. You were fast asleep."

"If I was asleep I could not hear you. Gotcha."

"That's a nice thing for you to do, Charlie. It's awful to be old, but to be old and alone and in bad health... It's, it's..."

"A surprise," said Marie.

Tallack's heart lifted. His wife made a joke.

"That's the wrong thing to say."

Marie picked at the nappy fabric of the couch. She glanced around the floor of the room as if she had dropped something.

Marie lifted her face to Tallack.

"Is he going soon?"

Mike gave Tallack a wink.

"Well," he said, "I promised Rene I'd come to his house for Shabbat, and if I'm late for lighting the candles he gets sort of ruffled feathers." It was barely three o'clock. Sunset was not for four hours.

Mike drained his glass to the bottom, till the ice cubes rattled. To make his enjoyment obvious he smacked his lips.

"Take care, darling." Mike kissed her on the cheek.

"Cold lips!"

Tallack followed Mike out to his car. Marie called "Don't leave me!" She struggled to rise from her chair but got no place.

"I'll be back, honey." By this time Marie trusted nothing and nobody.

"It is the damndest thing," Tallack was saying to Mike. "First she's sociable, then it is like she forgets all the rules of being with people. Dennis and his wife were over, and out of nowhere Marie starts talking to the girl about what kind of a build she has."

"Abigail got sick that same way. From all the pills and

whatever, I don't know what the hell, it was like a three-legged circus."

Watching Mike pull away from the curb Tallack felt two hundred years old.

Back in the house he found Marie had made it to her feet and was rummaging in the hall closet. She was desperate about it, pulling things down from the shelf and tossing them aside. Winter hats, a softball, an ancient bottle of crème de Cacao; Tallack hated the taste of it but for some reason they often received it as a present when people came over; along the way people had gotten the wrong idea.

Marie looked at the stuff in her hand for a moment, decided it was not what she wanted and dropped it.

"What are you doing, honey?" Tallack said, gentle as he could manage, what with everything.

"I want those Yellow Pages! I'm calling a psychiatrist. I need someone who can wash my head!"

"Honey, you don't need a psychiatrist." Tallack wrapped his arms around her but she would not be held.

"No, no, no! I'm crazy, Charles! Did you hear what I said to Mike? I know what comes out of my mouth!"

Dragging her in a bear hug across the room Tallack wrestled Marie to the sofa. Fat tears fell on his hands. She was wet with perspiration and smelled unclean; had she been aware of it she would have been mortified.

After a minute she lifted her chin enough to look Tallack in the eye.

"May I have a drink?"

"There's the iced tea left."

"Scotch, if you don't mind. With the cubes. I saw some in the closet."

"Scotch? I don't know what your doctor would have to say about that."

"What could it hurt?"

"You make a point."

Tallack poured two glasses, with plenty of ice for Marie. Bringing them back he found her stretched across the couch and deeply asleep. He got the big comforter with the entwined wedding rings on it Maureen gave them one year for Christmas. Marie seemed to disappear under it, she had gotten so small. The picture of this made Tallack uneasy.

By then Tallack was hungry. It was after four o'clock, not too early to call it dinner if you have not had lunch. He made spaghetti and drank both glasses of Scotch while the water was boiling.

"Happy landings,"Tallack said, lifting his glass to nobody.

Day into evening and Tallack had more to drink. The cushioning effect of alcohol on his head was welcome. Only a little drunk he sat just looking at Marie sleeping, unexpectedly content. He got the idea it would be good to read. He took a book from the little library they had—something about North American geology. He could not have said where he got such a book.

It was then that he thought of writing to Cynthia Hipsley.

Tallack's end of their letter writing was mainly limited to cards at Christmas and so on; some years he forgot even that. Women do not expect men to write letters and Tallack counted on that. "I'm sorry," he began, then started over because no one wants to hear that for an opener.

Marie has come down with some mystery illness the doctors can't name. It has preoccupied me.

Right now she is napping. I am beginning to accept that she will leave me one day, even if writing that out loud feels like the worst kind of jinx. I'm glad at least she can be at home until whatever happens happens.

Watching her asleep she looks awful tired. Not from the illness, I don't think, but from this long life. It feels to me you women are created to live better with details than men are, though maybe I think that because I am bad with details.

Among the reasons I like you, Cynthia, is that I imagine your life with out any details. In my imagination you never pour milk in your coffee and realize too late that it is curdled, you never forget to pay the light bill. I hope it is enough to say ~~I know it is not~~ I know that is not true. The thought of you (and face it the thought of you is what I have since 1945) allows me a life side by side with the one I got. A second life. If people are scrupulous that is what everyone would choose—a second life, just for the comparison's sake. (Did I get that line from you?) If I stayed in England and spent this life with someone else (!) Marie would have become that person for me. Perhaps I would be sitting beside another elderly woman watching her sleep and thinking these same thoughts, only with different characters and events in them.

I am not ready for the solitude that is coming.

I have always believed that every person is bursting at their seams.

Tallack fell asleep with his pad of paper on his lap. When he woke it was the deepest part of the night and far from dawn. The clock down the hall in the bedroom dinged the same note four times, quietly, for the record.

Silver light came in the window from the streetlamp. Tallack's idea of the afterlife was of a place illuminated in that kind of silver light, a place where nothing much happened and things were pretty quiet. A place where all the mysteries of life on earth were investigated and people spent their time in study.

While Tallack slept Marie had propped herself up on the couch. The blanket he had put around her was on the floor. When his head cleared Tallack's first thought was that Marie might be cold and he should do something about it. Her hands were palms up in her lap, as if she had made an attempt to grab the blanket back. Tallack realized she was staring at him.

"I'm lucid," she told Tallack.

"I'm glad, honey."

"I was afraid I died, Charles." She spoke in an even tone.

Tallack squeezed his eyes shut to force himself awake.

"I woke up. I didn't know what that red light was." She nodded at the cable box. "It looked like a church candle. I thought I might be in heaven. Then I saw you sitting there and I thought you were dead too. I thought it was over."

"Just dozing."

"My head aches so bad."

"The sky's already brightening. Why don't I help you to bed?"

"Did I fight with you, Charles? I was crying."

"Everything just caught up with you."

"You were going to get me a drink. Did I get it?"

"No, you fell asleep."

"Why didn't you wake me?"

"I would have needed dynamite."

Marie said, "All my life I never remember my dreams. Other people do. You do."

Marie said, "You have always had nice hands, Charles."

Written while tipsy or not, the next day Tallack did not alter a word of his letter to Cynthia when he left it for the postman except that he told himself to look up the spelling of the word *scrupulous* some time.

The solemn is companion to the commonplace.

Marie's last morning, August 29, 1993, she sat limp in an armchair. She was not asleep; more she was boneless. To put her in the cheerful sunshine Tallack pushed her chair nearer the front window. The expression on her face while she watched the street was absorbed; she looked alert.

There was big news from Shelly: she was pregnant with the baby who would turn out to be Abbie, Tallack's second granddaughter. Eileen told Tallack all about it when she came running into the house ahead of Shelly.

If Marie did not understand the news she registered the atmosphere of delight. Even Eileen could tell.

"Fine," Marie chuckled, rubbing her hands like someone expecting a wonderful treat. "This is nice to have."

That last morning Tallack was off to do the Home Visitors. Going out the door he turned to look at Marie.

"See you at lunch, honey." Loudly. Anyone would think deafness was Marie's problem. She was reaching her hands out to Eileen. She sang and Eileen danced:

Who is the man in the high black hat?
The high black hat and the sun at his back?
Who is the man in the high black hat
and the blade in his hand that goes whack, whack, whack?

This was wonderful. Not the ditty Marie was singing (which was alarming) but that she was singing at all. Sun poured in through the window and lit them both, Marie singing and Eileen doing a kind of jig. The sun's white light washed out the features in their faces.

That was a day so hot the sky seemed to shriek. At the hospital the cooling system in the kitchen was out and in the steaminess the smell of cooking was nauseating. One young man Tallack knew by sight pushed a tall cart of hot trays into the freight elevator. "This is awful," Tallack told him. The guy only stared back, unable to even move his head. Another woman, white smock over her orange sari, stood before a kettle stirring something souplike. She was just tall enough for the steam to drift across her face.

They gave Tallack a light rota that day, and when he returned someone mentioned that Mrs. Gascogne went home sick from the heat. Tallack saw her waiting at the bus stop in front of the hospital. There was no bench and so she stood on the shadeless sidewalk. She was holding a folded newspaper to the side of her head like someone defending against a blow.

"May I take you somewhere, Mrs. Gascogne?" Tallack asked. Her face was puffy with the beginnings of sunstroke. It appeared she was trying to place him.

"Oh," she said, "oh, thank you." Tallack could almost hear the blacktop bubbling on the street.

Mrs. Gascogne was so weak from the sun she had difficulty opening the car door. She bent herself into the front seat and fell back exhausted. Her clear brown skin, tight on her face, swam with freckles, beaded like the outside of a water glass.

"Twenty minutes waiting for that bus." Mrs. Gascogne fanned her face with the newspaper. "I was about to fall over."

"Where are we going?"

"I live on Presidents Street. You know where that is?"

"I've delivered lunches for you up there."

"My husband brought the car in today because the brakes were soft. I heard your wife was sick."

"She'll be OK.'

It was a long time since Mrs. Gascogne's neighborhood was called Niggertown, though for all practical purposes that is still what it was since nobody White seemed to live there. At the far end of Presidents Street were the Projects, three boxes four-stories high, painted white and lavender and pocked with rows and rows of small windows. (After it was opened the complex was nicknamed the Kolored Kremlin for a while, though not by anyone who lived there.)

On the side of an apartment block making one wall of an apartment block was a giant mural. Under the motto *Truth·Justice·American Way* the mural showed three muscled black women with good teeth, children flying kites and Martin Luther King Jr. In the lower left was a woman in a red and black gingham dress and a pink bonnet. A balloon above her head said *Sojourner Truth*. It was spectacular.

Standing in the street before Mrs. Gascogne's driveway was a collection of young men, not boys anymore and looking a little dazed about that. They were idle, waiting for something of interest to come along. One wore a headset and moved to music only he could hear, isolated. A conspiracy theorist would suppose the government handed out those radios or whatever they were to keep young dark-skinned men tractable.

Mrs. Gascogne's husband was in the driveway massaging his yellow car with a big sea sponge after its ordeal in the shop. He looked past his wife to Tallack.

Mrs. Gascogne had trouble getting to her feet and wobbled where she stood, holding on to Tallack's car door. "What did the garage tell you?" she said without preliminaries. Lots of good marriages eschew the phatic. That does not need to mean anything.

Tallack went around to the passenger side of the car and stood behind her, ready to assist.

"They tell me the car is straightened out."

The husband was not much taller than Tallack, younger but with white hair and tortoise shell glasses, in khaki slacks and a navy golf shirt. For a man merely washing his car he looked pretty good.

"Until Mr. Tallack came along I was getting sun-poisoned waiting for that bus. I'd be fine if I could have a glass of water." Mrs. Gascogne sounded awfully weak. "I need to get inside. Thanks again," she said, turning. She wanted Tallack to go.

"Glad to do it. I was coming over this way," as if that could possibly be true. For some reason he saluted.

Driving home Tallack could not shake the feeling that he had put his foot in it. Maybe her old man was jealous. The idea pleased Tallack—when was the last time he had made another man jealous? But when else do men, even old men, ever study each other except when there is a woman in the story? Tallack supposed another time would be when there was money on the table.

The uproar in his house was audible from the street. Inside the house Marie was sprawled half in a chair, half on the floor, hands slack in her lap, weeping. His whole life Tallack never heard crying like that, like the screeching of a terrified parrot, like a keening addressed to God directly.

Shelly was kneeling, trying to quiet Marie, pleading with her to calm down.

"What is it, mom? What is it, mom?"

Eileen watched from the doorway of the kitchen. When Tallack came in she yelled, "Papa's here!" the same way she might yell hooray. Tallack put his arm around Marie's shoulder and dried her eyes with his handkerchief.

"Don't you feel all right, honey?" At the sound of Tallack's voice Marie's face collected and her focus resolved on his face.

"What's happening to me?"

"Twenty minutes she's been like this," Shelly said.

"What do you need, Marie? What can I get?" Calm as could be.

Marie shook. Her head rolled, her eyes rolled.

Walking to the kitchen and snatching up Eileen on his hip in one motion Tallack said, "Grandma's going to be all right, honey. Come with me while I use the telephone."

Setting Eileen up on the kitchen counter Tallack telephoned Chand, whose number was taped to the wall beside the telephone. Tallack was grateful that the receptionist got him on the line quickly.

Chand did not ask many questions.

"Don't wait for an ambulance. Take her to the emergency-medicine department at the hospital. They'll be waiting. I'll phone."

Shelly helped Tallack get Marie on her feet and out to the car. Were she aware of it Marie would have been ashamed to think the neighbors might see her out in her nightdress, her husband and daughter-in-law dragging her across the lawn like she was loaded.

They eased Marie into the front seat and buckled her in. She said, very dignified, "I'd prefer to wait here."

It seemed they caught every light. At each one Tallack honked and rolled through. Marie was collapsed against the door. Only her seatbelt kept her from sliding in a heap to the floor.

Tallack saw the light blink off in her eyes.

White men in blue scrubs waited at the loading dock of the emergency-medicine department. Without a word they pulled Marie out of the car, unconscious, and lifted her onto a gurney. They pushed her up a concrete ramp. Between the automatic doors of the emergency room they shot off like kids pushing a wagon. Tallack had no idea what he was expected to do.

Tallack came into the ER. Patients waiting in different degrees of distress looked at Tallack, curious to know what his trouble might be.

One of the two men who wheeled Marie from the car was behind a green curtain with a tall Black doctor—a baby doctor, she could not have been thirty years old—using an electrical paddle to his wife's chest. Each time she applied it the paddle made a click click noise, making Marie flail like a marionette.

"Go for it!" shouted the other man. Tallack did not know if the guy meant Marie or the tall doctor. The doctor was panting, wrestling and losing.

Something beeping changed its tone.

Tallack looked and saw how Marie's head was thrown back at a sharp angle, mouth open in an ***0*** shape like someone frozen in mid shout.

Tallack had a distinct sense of energy leaving the room, as if an electrical current were switched off. It seemed the lights dimmed.

The tall doctor laid a hand on Marie's wrist. In that pose she looked like a doctor from a hundred years ago. She glanced at the clock on the wall.

"That's enough. Would you step over here, Mr. Tallack?"

Marie lay wide-eyed under a pink oxygen mask. Tallack's knees buckled at the sight of her. She looked like she had fallen off a roof. Her arms and chest were smeared with two colors of goo where she had been stuck with needles and wired to monitors, a red something sprayed on her neck like graffiti. Fuzzy blue spittle at the corners of her mouth. She made a small arching movement with her back and tried to suck in a breath. Tallack knew not to hope. She was already gone.

He took Marie's hand to steady himself. Her skin was already cold. Her mouth seemed to pucker, but really she had stopped breathing.

"I'm proud of you, honey." He brushed the hair off her face the same way he did in the old days.

Marie was 69.

A hospital social worker helped Tallack through the arrangements. There was a surprisingly uncomplicated routine to it. Still it took the better part of two hours.

The hospital asked to do an autopsy. The social worker said the hospital was part of a clinical study of something called "terminal lucidity."

"I'm sure there's a joke in there somewhere," Tallack said, "but no."

By the time Tallack was home the day's heat was diminishing. Johnny was waiting. Tallack asked Johnny where Shelly and Eileen were.

"They only just left."

"How's Eileen?"

"Crabby. She knows something happened to grandma. How are you doing, Pop?"

"Numb. Nothing."

Tallack saw Johnny out the door and sat down on the chair by the window. He quickly fell asleep.

When Tallack woke the time was only a little after ten. He was surprised to feel hungry. Out of all the things he might have felt the desire for food felt the least appropriate.

You feel what you feel, he told himself.

It took a moment for his head to clear of sleep. On the other side of the window screen a spotted moth was dancing in the dark. Now and then it flung itself at the screen. It did not wise up and fly away. It hung in there. It was not giving up.

Marie had not been reincarnated as a flying insect; Tallack was never given to mystical thoughts. He knew the moth was only attracted to the light from the lamp beside his chair. Just the same he was comforted by the moth.

Tallack did not want comfort.

Grief takes the shape it likes.

For the funeral Maureen flew from Texas by herself. The second night of the wake she made her way out to Ilkeston, arriving in the middle of the rosary straight from the train in a taxi.

Tallack, who was never much for saying rosaries, looked up and saw Maureen standing in the doorway of the viewing room, her pull bag beside her; the bag was red. She looked like somebody else's grown daughter, a tall, worn woman in a blue blazer, the skin around her mouth beginning to pucker; Maureen was in midlife. That night her hair, which she always wore gathered at the back of her head, had slipped in a pile to one side; as she grew older Maureen's red hair was becoming not grey but white, the same way Marie's did. Tallack admired how she never colored it. He took that for a sign of her confidence.

Maureen's eyes swept the room like she was counting the house. Apart from her brothers and their wives it was mainly a crowd of old women, including three of Aunt Mae's daughters—Mary, Annie and Margaret, each of them younger than Tallack by at least ten years. The sisters bent their heads in constant conversation among themselves, even through the prayers.

Delores Tresca from across the street was there. So was Christine Barcelona, without her husband Buddy; they both left after the praying was done. Mike Siperstein was by himself at the back, unaccustomed to wakes but turning out just the same.

Up by the casket Tallack stood with a priest from St. Martin's. He did not know Tallack any better than Tallack knew him. All the same the priest tried to say a few words about Marie.

"I never had the luck to know Mrs. Tallack," he began, which right away lost everyone in the room because they knew what was coming. "Several of you here tonight have told me stories about what a fine lady she was, and of course how much she gave for her family." The usual boilerplate he would say over a thousand dead women before he was through. Tallack did not hold it against the guy. These rituals never did anything for him. He simply wanted the whole thing finished. When his turn to die came Tallack hoped everyone would keep that in mind.

Maureen did not like it though. After praying the rosary she came and kissed her father, and almost in the same breath said in his ear, "Mom deserved better than that canned spinach."

"The guy probably has to do two of these every week. Leave him alone. How was the trip?"

"He could show more imagination. Trip was fine."

They talked about the funeral in the morning, about who had been asked to come, all to put off the necessity of having to look at her mother's corpse.

"Come see Mom," Tallack said. "I think she looks OK."

Maureen walked over and knelt. She crossed herself and bowed her head, careful not to look at Marie's face. With eyes closed she prayed. Tallack remembered that when Maureen was a baby she slept on her side, hands out in front of her as though she had fallen asleep making a prayer. Or making shadow puppets.

Raising her head Maureen looked to her left and for a long while studied her mother in the teak box. Marie's skin was waxen. In the box with her Tallack had put daisies from their backyard. They laid her out in a peach-colored dress he knew she liked. Her beads were twined in her fingers. The man at the funeral home brushed the hair from her eyes in a way she never wore it. Her hair was so fine that all her life she had trouble getting it to stay in place. It used to charm Tallack the way she was forever brushing it out of her eyes.

Maureen was crying. Dennis and Tallack settled her in a chair. The other mourners looked away.

Tallack said, "She was worn out, honey. It just shows."

Later Tallack was sorry this was the last look at their mother his kids ever had. He wished they had just buried her.

"There is no crime, and no sin;
there is only hunger."

Fyodor Dostoevsky
The Brothers Karamazov

We are surprised at the way things develop.

For some months after Marie died Tallack regularly woke up at night convinced that she was in the room with him, that this was not dreaming, that if he reached out he would touch her solid body. Sometimes he sensed that she was above the bed, floating like a cartoon ghost. If she were alive Tallack would have teased her for the lack of imagination.

After a while the apparitions or whatever they were stopped. As time passed it frightened Tallack to discover that his memory of Marie's face faded. If he closed his eyes she was not there anymore. There was only the blurry shape of some woman wearing clothes.

Marie went on being dead.

A year after Marie's passing Tallack had the idea to frame a photograph of her that he specially loved. It was taken on the day Johnny married Shelly. When this picture was taken Marie was just beyond the middle of her life, and how pretty she looked. She stands on the step of a muted suburban synagogue, Shelly behind her in a pale lavender gown and already showing the bump that meant baby Eileen.

Each night after saying his prayers Tallack stared at this photograph for a long moment. His idea was to reimprint her face on his brain while he slept.

Tallack's theory worked. The picture of Marie in his head became the way she looked in that wedding photograph, always smiling, always beautiful, always alive. He kept up this ritual until the last night of his life.

For himself, Tallack would miss Marie as a collection of absences that regularly caught him by surprise. Waking up in the mornings he would always miss her smell.

At Christmas that first year Tallack received a condolences letter from Cynthia.

> *So sad to have your news about Marie. I feel I knew her. You said little enough about her over the years but her place in anything you ever told me about was always visible to me if not to you perhaps.*
>
> *I am jealous of her, still, and not for reasons anyone besides you might know. Don't recall if I ever told you this (time tumbles on) but after Bert passed away four years ago I had a feeling that I made a mistake in letting him get away. I felt a wish to have a friend with me through life, who knew all about me. Not a very romantic feeling, is it? It is, though in a way I'm not used to imagining romantic feelings.*
>
> *I suppose we both, you and I, live now more than ever in what you call the 'second life'. (I have your letter of several weeks ago here in front of me. How sad it is, you are.)*

Tallack hated the tone of this letter, with its old person's tone of bemused gloom. Coming from Cynthia, Tallack found this disappointing.

Even once he was out of a wife Tallack saw how the world had been extravagant to him. Instead of being grateful Tallack was greedy for more. This was one revelation he had.

In that first winter after Marie passed away Shelly was so pregnant with Abigail Marie that she was big as a Volkswagen. By March of 1993 she was in her seventh month.

"I'll be glad when this kid arrives," she told Tallack. "Every time I sneeze my bladder opens."

Tallack had other things on his mind in those months. In that slow cold winter after Marie's death he was speculating about why his daughter Maureen ever considered marrying a man like Lou Rigali.

When they met, you know, Lou was fresh from dentist school and full of himself. He was boyish in that way that gets tiresome in a grown man. Instead of "self-absorbed" Tallack tried calling him "taciturn"; he actually looked it up to make sure he was using the word correctly. It is a word that covers a lot of ground but did not cover Lou Rigali.

Marie—she always called Lou the "the DDS" as a way of avoiding the need to say his name—Marie considered Lou beyond salvation. (Literally, she meant beyond salvation. She was raised a Christian with a belief in the possibility of salvation for everyone but, having lived a long time, knew this was not the way to bet.) Marie had objections to all the mates her children picked, now one comes to think about it. She only really ever changed her mind about Shelly. And Shelly needed to produce Eileen to pull that off. Some sort of psychology, that was all Tallack could conclude.

Even grandchildren could not soften Marie toward the DDS. She barely saw those kids after Lou prevailed on Maureen to move to Houston, where he had heard dentistry prospects were better. Marie might fly there in winter to see them all but not Tallack; he did not like to travel. Tallack seldom saw Maureen's two boys and the result was he was never sure of their names; in his head he referred to them as Manny and Moe. Marie described what she had seen of those two adolescents as "unencouraging." They were liars who stole from their mother's purse. For their bad character Marie blamed the DDS entirely.

The girlfriends were the worst of it. Lou Rigali was the sort of married man who had girlfriends—"tootsies," Marie called them, a word which for Tallack brought to mind chorus girls. The word did not feel hard enough for the harm Lou caused. Then that winter after Marie's death Lou found a tootsie who inspired him to leave Maureen. He took an apartment with this tootsie on the opposite side of Houston. Manny and Moe were of an age to be consulted. They picked the no-good father. Their new home was an hour away, far enough to be a headache when Maureen needed to visit.

"To hell with Lou," Tallack said on the phone when she told him. He immediately wished he could take it back. You want your kids to be able to talk to you, and no one wants to be told their romantic choice was obviously idiotic all along.

Maureen met Lou when she had already been through two serious boyfriends (that Tallack remembered). Neither showed interest in marriage and Maureen moved on. Marriage was what she wanted. She was so eager for it, Tallack recalled thinking, that it was spoiling her personality. He even remarked this to Marie after Maureen told them she was marrying Lou Rigali.

"I thought girls gave up on marriage." He had read that.

"They have," Marie said. "But they're stuck." Marie always represented herself as a skeptic on marriage—puzzling, naturally, to Tallack, her husband. Marie was affectionate but never sentimental. She liked romantic movies, say, but did not believe them for a moment.

Tallack was in attendance, for example, when her friend Barbara Riordan told Marie she was engaged. Instead of congratulations Marie said, "Isn't there time for that? Cripes, Barbara, life will be passing you by before you're even on your way." Barbara was a tall girl who was shy about her height.

"Yeah," Barbara told her, "but I want kids and I need to get out of the house. My mother runs me nuts."

"You be careful or you'll end up like her."

Later on the subway home Tallack asked, "Was all that stuff with Barbara aimed at me?"

"Not you, Charles. You're lovely."

Tallack wondered how much of this mixed feeling Marie transmitted to Maureen, and what effect it might have had on Maureen's—on her *expectations* of Lou Regali.

Tallack was never to Maureen's house in Houston. After the marriage ended he pictured it empty, his daughter passing like a shadow among the echoing rooms, an unfurnished place where she rued the day. He saw it enormous in what he imagined was the Texas style, as if Maureen had married a country-music star and not Lou Rigali. (Then Tallack thought about Syd Barrett, and the way Syd used to tease him about owning oil wells back in America.)

It was puzzling to Tallack that Maureen seemed all right about the end of her marriage to the DDS.

"I don't mind being solitary. Before I was."

"Even when you were my tiny baby girl?"

"Pardon?"

"Were you?"

"Sure, Pop—isn't everyone? If they weren't no one would marry anybody. They would have the babies and move along."

Every day Tallack passed a photo hanging in the hallway of his house showing Maureen on a swing. It was never out of its frame but he knew that on its back *Maureen–age 2* was written in pencil, by Marie or by him, he could not recall. The picture was taken at the Dana Middle School over the back fence from their house. Baby Maureen in a little winter coat, hat buttoned under her chin so that all you could see was the chubby face laughing, delirious. Marie's arm intruding on the frame, pushing. Tallack must have held the camera; he sees his shadow in the shot.

When Maureen was that age Tallack liked to stand outside her bedroom in the mornings listening to her in the crib saying all the words she knew, stopping to clap for herself and say "Yey!" Tallack liked her for that. It physically hurt him to imagine pain ever coming to his girl.

There is a temptation for people old as Tallack was old to lament the present. Corn and strawberries were sweeter, they say, winters were colder, people were kinder. Generally Tallack kept that tendency in check. When Marie was alive it was easier to do. She had the knack of simply denying the intrusion of anything unpleasant.

Race riots, price rises, childhood cancers, an upswing in violent crime?

"It doesn't bear thinking about," Marie would say—while she gobbled up the details as if it were the gossip of a seedy ex-movie star. Especially if it were the gossip of a seedy ex-movie star.

"Most people just want to raise their kids and get along," she might say. "Don't you think?" What Tallack thought was that by the end of her life Marie could not sustain this faith.

A year or so before she died Marie said to Tallack in some context, "I used to be able to find a little of myself in even the most terrible people."

"And now?"

"Not so much now."

If we could we would own everything.

It was 1996, late winter, not three years after Marie passed away. On St. Patrick's Day Shelly phoned Tallack to say she had an appointment with her obstetrician—would he mind collecting Eileen from the nursery school? It would be his pleasure, Tallack told her, that as it happened he had some free time.

Tallack left his car at home. The afternoon was perfect—sunny and cold outdoors, no wind, the sky empty, only a sort of pale haze up there. He could feel the world shining on his face. A little snowfall from the previous day left a dusting on things, enough to cheer up the view. March is the dullest month and it was good to have weather.

Tallack's finger bones were cold as he walked. He shoved his hands deep into his coat pockets. On the way up Buttonwood Street he met Delores Tresca out walking her dog Silas.

Tallack had not seen Delores since before Christmas.

Silas made to jump up on Tallack's chest, but by then he was an old dog and his jumping days were over. He wagged his tail and seemed to grin, really pleased to see Tallack. Man's best friend.

Tallack patted the dog's head.

"I'd begun to think you'd moved away without telling me." The previous September Delores stuck a "For Sale" sign on her front lawn. It was still there.

"I'd never do that. I was up in Massachusetts visiting Donny. And his wife."

Like Tallack in those days the first thing Delores did when she stopped moving was to search her pockets for a cigarette. She was still dressed for snow in a paisley wool skirt that covered the tops of her red leather boots. Her long white hair was tucked up under a furry Cossack hat.

"It snowed nearly every day," she said. Tallack was aware of Delores' face. An old face, the flesh relaxed, a good face that must have been attention-getting once. Tallack did not recall attending one way or another to Delores or her face when she was a young mother in the neighborhood. What he remembered was her marching door to door signing people up for or against some cause, hair down her back, ready for an argument if that was what you wanted.

"You wear your hairdo different," he told Delores. "It's becoming to you."

"French braid. My daughter-in-law suggested it."

"What's happening on the house?"

"The market is soft, the realtor tells me, or wait till spring. Or something." Silas sat on the edge of the curb, happy to get off his feet while Delores had a chat. The dog looked around the street with an air of ownership, pleased with things on Buttonwood Street.

"If you sold the house where would you go?"

"I like it up where Donny lives. It's pretty. There are plenty of trees. Silas would enjoy that." At the sound of his name the dog perked up. He *would* enjoy that.

"What will you *do* was my question."

Delores shrugged. "Bank the cash or go to the land beyond the sky. My preference is to bank the cash."

Delores lived without her husband Alen far longer than Tallack had been without Marie. Tallack presumed she was more used to it. Tallack missed being married, a separate feeling from missing Marie. Being married gave walls and floors to his existence, kept the world at its proper distance. While the earth went through its phases—wars, elections, the vogue for some movie star, social whatnot—Tallack observed it all with interest but was detached from it at the same time.

Two years later with Marie gone everything was turned on its head. Tallack was learning to see how constant the world was in its alterations, and how changeable his part was, if that makes sense.

Marie said to Tallack once in the years between selling the store and her dying that she was teaching herself to like solitude. She said this after coming in from a walk in which she encountered Alen Tresca from across the street. He invited himself to join her, and this broke her meditative mood.

Marie and Alen were coming down Buttonwood Street when they met one of the neighbors, a Serbian whom Tallack never spoke to that he recalled. The man had only minutes before learned that his wife was leaving him. When he came out of his house he was in a daze of immediate bad news. His heart was split open.

"I never saw anyone actually tear their hair," she reported.

"The wife is gone permanently?"

"Gone to his sister's—*his* sister's."

"Other people's married lives are amazing."

"You find that?"

"I will not ask why the sister."

"Does it matter? The poor guy is desolate."

"Or his house is, in the sense of, you know, uninhabited."

"But not him."

"Sorry?"

"I don't think he was really so crazy about the wife. To hear him speak of her, I'm saying. I think he's just frightened about how he'll manage the loneliness. I could feel that coming off him. I recall," Marie said, "I recall your mother liked to say people get married thinking it is a cure for solitude, but on the contrary."

"Even once I never heard my mother say that."

"It is an expression."

"You can't be sure. It might have been an outburst." For the rest of his days Tallack missed Marie every day.

Memory is more than recollection.

It was 1:30 in the afternoon, an odd hour of the day when only infants and doddering retirees were abroad.

The trees were bare. There was something in the quality of the light that reached into Tallack. Spring waited in the wings. Tallack sniffed the warming up, sweetness in it that made him hungry. He said to himself the air smelled lubricious, a good word for the wet, fertile smells of life awakening.

From lack of exercise his bones creaked and his brain was full of spooks. In life he had met people, not by any stretch old as him, who spent so much time alone that the interior of their heads got to be a house of mirrors. Otherwise Tallack was in such good health that some days he feared he might live forever.

The shoulder of the road where Tallack walked was muddy. He wore a pair of bad-weather shoes Dennis and Diane gave him at Christmas. Those shoes made him feel like a kid the way they let him walk anywhere, splash through puddles if he felt like it. Second childhood, he thought, always on the lookout for signs of senility creeping in.

Walking past the Peking Dragon, Ilkeston's chop-suey restaurant, Tallack looked in at the staff sitting around a table playing cards, their jackets draped on chair backs. By the cash register the hostess perched on her stool watching the street. When Tallack looked in she met his eye. Tallack smiled at her but the woman turned away.

After that place opened Eileen had nightmares about the scaly red dragon painted on the front window; between its teeth the dragon held the Earth. After a while Eileen pestered her parents to take her there; Tallack always admired the way Eileen was never afraid of anything for long. This never changed even after she was a grown woman and things had happened to her.

Once when Tallack was minding her he took Eileen to the Peking Dragon for lunch.

"I like China," she told her grandfather. "I want us to move there." She had no concept of China being far away.

"What could you do in China?"

"I could have a restaurant."

"That might work. You'd be a capitalist."

"What's that?"

"Someone who has a business."

"Like Terry."

Terry ran the Little Kids childcare, where Eileen spent her days while her parents worked. Tallack could never recall Terry's last name, if he ever knew it. She was in school with his daughter Maureen; he recalled that Terry used to be around their house quite a lot. Long straight hair down her back, parted precisely in the middle of her skull, a flowered dress down to her bare feet. He recalled picking up Eileen at Little Kids once and Terry wearing a red and black button on her duffel coat that said

VAGINAL
PRIDE

Terry was divorced and needed to support herself, which led her into the kid business. Tallack got all this from Eileen. She considered herself chummy with Terry.

Eileen was waiting for her grandfather. The "school" was in a converted hardware store with plenty of room for the children and a large plate-glass window that let passersby peak in at the pandemonium. In front of this window Eileen was sitting on a bench with another boy and the boy's father, a short man with a dark face. The father was watching (morosely, Tallack thought) while Eileen and his son compared the contents of their backpacks. The father wore ear buds on a wire that disappeared into the Walkman clipped to his belt.

Tallack thanked the man for waiting.

"Where's Terry?" he asked this guy.

"Inside." The man whistled for his son to come along.

"Terry's going to the doctor," Eileen said after they were gone. "Her knee hurts."

"She should not have let you wait by yourself."

"I wasn't by myself."

Eileen used to be a chatterbox. Walking past the shops of Ilkeston Park she stopped in front of every window to comment on the merchandise. She liked the hardware-and-appliance dealer. She asked her grandfather to explain what the products in the windows did.

Eileen's favorite stop (to Tallack's delight, naturally) her favorite was the place where Guys & Gals used to be, where the Tenutta family built their two-story "mini mall." Eileen had the idea Guys & Gals used to occupy the whole edifice. She loved the thought of Guys & Gals and repeated Tallack's stories about running the shop, as if by repeating them she could make a role for herself in their telling.

"Remember the time you had the fire, and Grandma put it out because you burned your hands?"

"Remember the time my dad got mixed up handing out the school uniforms and all the kids had to come back?"

"Remember you were working all night and the policeman came in with his gun because he thought you were a robber?"

"Remember when you were in the movie that was on TV?"

Those, Tallack told her, were the days.

They made a game of stamping footprints in the snow. Tallack planted his big shoe in the powder and Eileen placed her little foot in the print. She laughed every time and rubbed out the marks they made.

They walked past the Ilkeston Public Golf Course. Tallack was raised in upper Manhattan. For people like him golf never came up. But one year the Masters champion, Cary Middlecoff, gave an exhibition at the course. For some reason Maureen, who was not even ten years old at the time, decided she had to go. She liked saying Middlecoff's name and she knew he was famous for something.

The exhibition was on a Saturday afternoon, the busiest day of the week at Guys & Gals, but Tallack did not like to disappoint his daughter. In those days Marie was still home with the boys so Rolfe Tenutta (who was never completely comfortable running the shop on his own) Rolfe took over while Tallack brought Maureen up to the big match. She liked it, walking the course with the gallery and hearing the silence that descended each time the players hit shots. But she was only a little girl. After nine holes she was all worn out.

It was when they were passing the golf course that Eileen declared she had seen Marie the night before.

"Where did you see her?"

"I didn't see her but I knew she was there. She was in my room. She pulled up the blankets on my bed."

"I have that feeling in our house too. Like Grandma and your dad and Uncle Dennis and Aunt Maureen are still living there."

"Yeah. Grandma is a ghost. I spin around and she *disappears* quick as a wink."

"Friendly ghosts."

"I'm afraid Grandma's cold. Ghosts are cold."

"Grandma's not a ghost, honey. All you have to do is think about her and she's there."

"Grandma's in the ground. She's all bones."

It was all right to be talking this way to Eileen. Tallack did not have to explain so much to a child, or elaborate his feelings so that they sounded more complicated than they were. Walking in the cold sunshine only made him think of life, and of how much Marie would have enjoyed it.

This was the day when his trouble began.

Dark houses breed misery.

They were down the road from the Ilkeston hospital when a car shot past. Its radio thumped like something trying to jump out of a box. Even with the car's windows rolled up the vibration of the winter air was considerable.

The car was the yellow Camry Mrs. Gascogne's husband—Mrs. Gascogne from the hospital—was washing the day Tallack gave her a lift home, the day Marie died. In the wide driveway of a big house on Charlotte Road the car turned around and came back for Tallack and Eileen.

Mrs. Gascogne pulled up and rolled her window down.

"How about a lift, Mr. Tallack?" Mrs. Gascogne gave Eileen a big smile. "You must be frost-bit." Mrs. Gascogne shivered in sympathy.

"Eileen and I are out for a walk. We like the cold, don't we, honey?"

"I'm freezing, Papa."

Mrs. Gascogne pulled her seat forward to let them climb in back. She introduced the young man at the wheel as her son Mitchell.

"Mitchell, this is Mr. Tallack." Tallack surmised that

Mitchell had charge of the music selection. Eileen rocked to the music, side to side. She liked it even though the singer sang angry, angry like the bomp bomp beat behind him. Tallack was not so old that he could not understand that anger was the *point.* It was the frantic kind of beat television plays to accompany scenes of burning buildings.

I'm the wrong man
Take you when I want
Better let me
Be smart
Fun facts
Or leave outta here

What the hell is that? Tallack wondered, and almost out loud.

Mrs. Gascogne turned around in her seat.

"Mitchell got me from work today." She shouted to be heard above the radio. "My car's been in the shop."

"Again?"

"What?" She tipped an ear toward Tallack.

"The day I took you home last summer the car was in the shop."

"Mitchell, turn down the radio."

"Face it, mommy, this car's a piece of shit."

"Don't use words like that in front of the little girl, Mitchell."

"Sorry, little girl." Mitchell and Eileen smiled at each other in the mirror.

They were turning into Buttonwood Street.

"Mitchell's just come from getting his union card. He's training a year for a mason."

"Apprenticing, mommy, not training. Not like I'm a boxer."

Tallack looked at Mitchell's hands on the steering wheel. They were long and thin, and the wrists were small. More what you would picture the hands of a pianist than a mason. For masonry Tallack supposed a man needed more skill than strength, more like billiards or some other sport where talent mattered more than force.

"Maybe I'll be your first customer." Now Tallack was shouting over the music too. "I've been trying to figure out what to do with the bricks from my front steps. Can masonry rot?"

"No," Mitchell said over his shoulder. "The cement freezes and thaws, expands and contracts. How old is your house?"

"I'm not sure. Fifty years?"

"That's probably your answer."

At Tallack's house Mrs. Gascogne insisted (over Mitchell's unspoken reluctance) that they all get out and have Mitchell give a professional opinion of Tallack's front steps. Inevitably his opinion was discouraging.

"Your bricks are in good shape," he said, "but the mortar wasn't intended to hold so long. Look how it's spalled. I mean," he said, like only an idiot could overlook the fact, "I mean think of all the people who put their weight on these steps in—what did you say this house was?"

"Sixty years, I think."

"It has to happen. Think of all the winters."

Eileen loved this. She was interested in home repairs and

do-it-yourself jobs. And she liked the novelty of new people around. She squatted beside Mitchell and watched him while he bent to rock the two loosest bricks in the crumbling steps of Tallack's old house, jiggling them like an orthopedist does to your bones.

"Fix these first. Somebody'll crack their head. Wait until the weather gets warmer."

"Papa's driveway is cracked." Eileen pointed.

"We don't have to tell people all my secrets, Eileen."

"Mitchell, come look." Mrs. Gascogne, led by Eileen, was already halfway across the snowy lawn. Mitchell looked at Tallack and they exchanged smiles. They were humoring the women and this gave them common ground for a moment.

Eileen knelt on the driveway and brushed the snow away with her blue mitten.

"There it is!" Eileen pointed at the gray crack that had been there nearly three years. Mitchell squatted to study it. It was almost five and the late-winter light was going from the sky. Tallack's toes were cold. To keep his blood moving he was doing a sort of dance.

"I thought it was lightning," he told Mitchell.

"Won't hurt if you leave it. It's not doing you any harm."

Mentally Tallack crossed it off his list.

While they deliberated Christine Barcelona came home. She got out of her car with bags of groceries. She set the bags on the hood of her blue Volvo and pretended to fiddle with her keys, all the while watching what went on in Tallack's driveway. When the others bent to examine the crack Tallack acknowledged Christine with a wave. She nodded.

"Papa, I'm cold."

"Better get up off your knees, honey."

Tallack invited Mitchell and Mrs. Gascogne to come inside for tea. Mrs. Gascogne declined, which Tallack was relieved to hear because his house was a mess.

"My husband gets his dinner 6:30 on the dot," said Mrs. Gascogne.

"He's a privileged man."

"I get something out of it. Very nice to meet you, Eileen."

"Good-bye. Good-bye, Mitchell." Mitchell smiled.

Once the Gascognes drove off Christine headed indoors. Lights switched on within her dark house.

Eileen was always hungry and Tallack made egg salad. At that time it was almost the only thing she would eat. Tallack found egg salad disgusting to look at and awful to smell. That he fixed it up for Eileen was proof of his love.

Later they watched the early evening news. The local TV station ran a consumer-affairs segment Eileen did not like to miss.

At six-thirty Johnny and Shelly came from the obstetrician's and collected Eileen. They were only there a moment. After that, Tallack had the whole evening to himself.

Feeling a little lonely Tallack telephoned Maureen in Texas. No one was home down there so he called Dennis. Tallack heard in the way Dennis answered that he was distracted.

"Diane just went to bed," he said. "We took the day off from work and drove up to Connecticut. She wanted to go to some special nursery for flowers." Tallack knew his son was being loyal by not making a wisecrack about the special flowers. As it was for his father the pleasure Dennis took in flowers was more general than differentiated.

There was a little pause and over the telephone the noise of the television playing in the room with Dennis. "Diane just went to bed."

"You mentioned. Are you OK?"

"I'm fine, Pop. Just enjoying the quiet."

"I'm rooting for you." Tallack did not know why he said that, but it felt like it made sense.

Going to bed that night Tallack was thinking, My poor boy. Dennis and Diane felt the absence of children in their house, and every year the absence got bigger. No one could tell them, Get over it. Their lovemaking must have been grim, everything focused on making the biology click click. Doubly frustrating since most people seemed to do that trick so easily, even accidentally.

Sitting on the edge of the bed pulling off his shoes Tallack's eye fell on the photograph of Marie taken the day Johnny married Shelly, the one he kept to remind him of what Marie looked like. Tallack did not need reminding of what it felt like waiting for her to come to bed, the way she smelled of Ivory soap. Tallack washed with that stuff, too, to have her smell around him. Her skin warm when he pressed his face to it, cool when he flipped up the blouse of her pajamas and touched her with his hand. They were both light sleepers. If in the middle of the night Marie got up to use the toilet Tallack was always alert when she came back to bed.

"Ruffle me," she would say. The dead of night became the center of everything.

Tallack wished that for Dennis.

"Ruffle me."

At the time this appeared to be just one more day, one more thrown on the pile.

We cannot control what people think.

It was a housebound Saturday, rainy, warm for the end of winter. The last of the cheery snow was melted. The pale green grass was coming back. Hope hope hope.

Tallack was inspired to clean his house. He spent the morning taking newspapers and junk mail to the blue recycling bin in back of his house. He emptied his dishwasher and put everything away. He vacuumed the three bedrooms, including the one he referred to as the guest room, though Tallack never had guests.

Now Tallack was in his kitchen making lunch. Out in the living room the television was on to create a little noise in the house, a little reference to other humanity.

Tallack tuned to the same channel for hours; he did not care enough to change it. First a news show featuring topics of interest to Hispanic viewers, then a western about a troubled friendship between a cowboy and an Indian that ends sort of bittersweet with the cowboy planning to marry his gal. After this a sports cavalcade. The TV passed the hours with him.

About three o'clock the doorbell rang. Tallack was surprised to find Buddy and Christine Barcelona on his front steps. Christine wore a quilted pink jacket, yellow umbrella open over her head. Buddy wore a sweater. He was wet and looked unhappy about it.

Christine said, "Charles—got a minute?"

"I didn't know it was raining. Come in." She shook out her umbrella on the front steps.

"How could you not know?" Christine asked.

Tallack was assuming they were collecting for something—Easter Seals or whatever. He was aware of looking squalid. All over the floor were newspapers from the previous three days spread around the one big chair in the room, which is where Tallack sat watching the television when he ate. On a stack of newspapers was the plate from the previous night's sandwich.

"I'm getting ready to paint," Tallack said.

Buddy sat himself on Tallack's couch, straight and impatient, a man who came to talk business and had no use for preliminaries. Christine unzipped her yellow jacket and sat beside him.

"Ever think about selling this place?" Buddy asked. Tallack misunderstood this as small talk.

"All the time. This house is falling apart faster than I am."

"You might get a good price."

"If someone was foolish enough to buy it they could have this house tomorrow."

"I heard Delores Tresca was offered three-ninety for her house," Christine said. She had heard no such thing, as Tallack knew. Delores would have gone like a shot had someone made an offer like that.

"Three-ninety! Marie and I paid $16,000."

"The appreciation's been tremendous in these houses," Buddy explained.

"Delores told me the other day no one's shown any interest in her house."

"*Are* you thinking about selling?" Christine asked.

"If I had brains I might be."

Buddy shifted in his seat and looked at the television. A tiny gymnast cartwheeled off a balance beam on the TV screen. She made a bad landing but threw her hands up in the air just the same. That is what they do.

"My sister Regina's had her eye on this house," Buddy said, "for her and her husband."

"Are you serious?"

"Yep," Buddy told him, like Gary Cooper. "Yep."

"I've heard Regina talk about it," Christine added brightly, like someone sharing a happy secret.

The TV somehow moved on from gymnastics to a kids' dance show and the music would not be ignored. "I grouse a lot," Tallack said, switching the TV off, "but I'm not really thinking about it. Not really."

"I saw you showing it to those people yesterday afternoon. The ones I saw you with. When I came home."

"What people?"

"There was a couple. You were with your granddaughter."

"Eileen."

"Yes."

"You mean Mrs. Gascogne and her son?" The light blinked on in Tallack's head. It did not take much to flip the switch. He was an insightful guy.

"Worried?" he asked.

"Not worried," Christine told him.

"Those people are my friends."

Buddy sighed the sigh of an exasperated man.

"Nobody's worried, Charles. I do not give a shit who you sell your house to."

"Those people who were here were your friends?" Christine stuck to the subject.

"That's what I said." Tallack walked to the far side of the room to follow his anger. He picked up the dirty plate and the newspapers and began a general tidying of the living room so he would not need to sit looking at the Barcelonas.

"All we're telling you is that Regina and Carl are looking for a house," Buddy said. "You've got a buyer on the hook." If it means anything Buddy had a small skull. He had no brains.

On the lamp table under *Time* magazine Tallack found a cereal bowl with petrified GrapeNuts stuck to its bottom. Tallack scraped the bowl experimentally with a thumbnail; GrapeNuts attach like barnacles to things.

"And if I were I'd sell it to the highest bidder—whoever had the most money."

The subject was closed, though they batted it around another 15 minutes. Tallack insisted he was not going anywhere. Buddy repeated that he did not care whether Tallack went anywhere or not. Christine asked where he thought he might move.

All the while Tallack was marching in and out of the living room, bringing dishes to the kitchen. Through with that he piled newspapers by the back door for the recycling. Tallack plumped the one pillow on the other end of the couch from where Buddy sat with Christine. The pillow had a tiger printed on it.

Tallack was on the point of spray waxing the dining-room table when the Barcelonas finally left. They were in a snit but Tallack had gotten a fair amount accomplished. His place looked a lot better.

For even allowing such people to sit in his house Tallack's conscience was troubled by a sense of having betrayed Mrs. Gascogne.

New life commands our wonder.

It was the first of April. Shelly was two weeks overdue; everyone—the doctor included—was resisting the idea of a caesarian. The way things played out she went into labor with Abbie the day after her forty-third birthday.

On that day Abbie was born Johnny telephoned. Tallack was in the kitchen microwaving cold coffee.

"What's the situation there?"

"We have several situations here," Tallack answered.

"Can I call on your babysitting skills for Eileen today? Shelly's ready to go to the hospital."

"Why are you gabbing? I'll be right over."

"The contractions are far apart. Her obstetrician thinks it will be a long labor but she'd like to have Shelly in the hospital." Tallack was up on his feet pouring his coffee down the sink.

"Stop talking, Dennis." Tallack washed his filthy eyeglasses under the tap.

Tallack was smiling. The baby was coming. New life in the family would be good. For some while Tallack had been feeling that Eileen was lonely by herself. As if to make this point she was sitting on the front steps, all solitary, when Tallack got to the house.

"You look morose."

"Mama's inside."

Shelly was leaning against the wall of the dining room, wan and a little goofy around the eyes.

"I was trying to meet you at the door just to see if I could do it," Shelly said. "I could not."

"I'm sorry it hurts, honey."

"Phew!" Shelly put her hand across her belly and for a moment went silent, eyes closed. She grabbed the arms of a chair and sat. Johnny appeared with a bag of her overnight things, said "Hi, Pop" as he disappeared into the kitchen and bustled around in there. There was the jingle of keys.

"I'll take the bag, Johnny. Help Shelly out to the car."

Eileen would not talk to her mother. Shelly crooned to her, "Gimme a little kiss, will ya, huh?" Shelly was listing dangerously and it was brave of her to be funny. Sighing with the resignation of a much older person Eileen stood and allowed Shelly to kiss her cheek.

"Be a good girl for Papa. Maybe I'll bring home a sister." Eileen would never admit she was appeased. Shelly waved when they drove off, but Eileen would not look.

"Don't worry about your mama, honey," Tallack told her.

"I won't."

For lunch Tallack made the inevitable egg salad. He reheated the morning's coffee a second time.

Eileen still did not have much to say but she was coming out of it. Her chin drooped at the table. Instantly she was in deep sleep. Tallack lifted her and carried her down the hall to his own bed. She was a dead wight in his arms, a substantial girl.

A bit past two o'clock the telephone went. Expecting to hear Johnny's voice Tallack grabbed it on the first ring. It was Mike Siperstein calling from St. Petersburg.

"Hello, Charlie—what do you hear from the kids?"

"Babies come when they choose, Mike. You know that."

"Boy, do I. Shelly and Rene both took two days getting here. With both of them Abigail had the back labor. Rene called me before. He did not know if I'd heard the word of it. Johnny already got to me."

"Why wasn't my son with his wife instead of making phone calls to people?"

"He told me they were getting her ready. I don't like thinking about it."

Mike paused. The quiet was a little awkward.

"Eileen's here taking a nap."

"How's she doing with all the excitement?"

"She seems a little thrown by the whole business. She gets it and she doesn't, I think."

"I was like that too," Mike told him, "even when I was the father. Got it and did not got it."

"How's the Florida weather?"

"Today's raining. It's too hot already for the beginning of April. I don't even go to the golf course."

"That's only because you're still used to the weather up here."

Mike's pause made Tallack wonder if he had said the wrong thing.

"With my jewelry business it's not so bad. That's indoors and you're air-conditioned. You could be living in any time of the year."

Again Mike stopped himself.

"Listen, Charlie, don't tell the kids because I haven't settled my mind on this score, but I'm thinking of moving back home."

"But it snows here."

"I'll take the snow. You can play only so much golf."

Down the phone line Tallack heard Mike take a breath. Tallack pictured him in the probably naked rooms of his condo. He had a hard time imagining other people's furniture.

"You've always made it sound nice."

"Who needs 'nice'? Without your relations and the scenery that brings up your memories you don't make a home. But keep it under the hat for now, OK? First I need to unload this place."

Eileen was weeping in her sleep. It was not anything to worry about; when they were small all the Tallack kids did that. Her whole life Tallack's mother did it, and she was a grown woman. Two, three in the morning—*heeyy, heeyy,* a sound like that—even at seven or eight years old Tallack would go and sit on the edge of her bed until she quieted. An experience of that nature leaves shadows behind.

Giving in to a craving for sweets (a craving which grows on older people in their later years, there should be a study) instead of lunch Tallack unwrapped a slice of cake he took home from the deli a few days before.

With the cake and a cigarette he went out on his front stoop sniffing the fragrance of harvested lawns. The air smelled humid, yeasty, exactly the smell of bread rising. He knew the word for this fragrance: petrichor. The sun was big and kind, and the birds made a happy racket, singing like a TV ad for carpet cleaner. The bricks in the top step still wobbled.

Tallack collected the newspaper off the driveway and read the headline about a fire in Detroit killing 17 people the day before. A terrible thing, but not, at least, an end-of-civilization story like the one below it:

Newborn In Dumpster

At 10 o'clock the telephone rang in Tallack's kitchen. Eileen had a sister. She was given the name Abigail after Shelly's mother.

Unhappiness is poverty.

Soon after Abbie was born Tallack tried to write a letter to Cynthia. Writing anything was hard because he was unused to it. He was sitting in his TV-watching chair, which he had moved to the window to give him a vantage on the street. So many blossoms popping, the atmosphere sugared. It would not be long now before the warm weather.

It was a night, probably April. Preparing for bed Tallack spotted a dried dribble of coffee down the stubble of his chin that had probably been there all day. Some days being very old made him laugh out loud. Other days it did not at all.

Across the street Delores Tresca stood at her front window and telephoned Tallack. He picked up on the fourth ring. Like all of us he worried when the phone rang after eight p.m.

"An hour ago I put Silas out on the steps and now he's gone. Would you mind driving me around? I don't see well at night."

Ten minutes later Tallack was at her door. With Silas.

"He was lying on my front lawn," Tallack told her. "He

looked like he had things to think over."

Delores took the dog's snout in her hands and pretended to be sharp with him. Silas wagged his tail and dipped his head apologetically at the same time.

"You're too old to be running around town."

Delores straightened, and when she did she observed Tallack register the smell of Scotch on her breath. Her face was flushed, although that may have been the coming up quickly.

"I was fixing a cocktail when I realized the dog was gone. Will you come in a minute?"

Delores was not in any way looped. She was relaxed. Wearing a red sweatshirt with a picture of that dog Snoopy on it she was still on the right side of the place where the lips and tongue tingle. That was Tallack's stopping point for drinking alone. Past that and he grew too melancholy and unable to think straight about anything.

Delores was in the kitchen pouring whisky for herself and Tallack. He stood in the frame of her kitchen doorway.

"I'm trying to recall the last time I was in this house," Tallack said. "It had to be before Alen died. I have a memory of helping him carry in a carpet remnant he was putting down in your basement. Silas was only a pup and he was yapping at all the commotion."

"Silas was or Alen?"

Delores cracked the ice-cube tray on the edge of the kitchen countertop. There was the sound of ice bouncing on Formica. She filled up a juice glass with ice and Scotch and handed it to Tallack. There must have been a half pint of whisky in it.

"Come sit down," Delores said.

Nothing Delores owned was new but the things she accumulated in life were interesting to rest eyes on. Over the couch was a big print of blue and pink paint dripping. Beside the couch was a pine-wood table with family pictures on it. Alen, the boys Donny and Raymond, several grandchildren, Delores when she was a bride and looking young.

Tallack was distracted by an idea that women are more equipped by their upbringing for the day they go it alone. It is in their training to know how to keep the places they live cheered up.

Delores set her drink on the edge of the little table next to the couch, the one with the crowd of photographs.

"Any action on this house yet?" Tallack asked.

"Not a peep. My house is so unloved." A pause hung in the air a moment, and Tallack drank.

"All of a sudden I find I'm lonely," Delores said. "I swan about these rooms at night pretending there is something I need to do with my evenings. It gets on Silas' nerves, the way I'm up and down and up and down. No wonder he took off tonight." The dog lifted his head when Delores spoke his name, wondering if he was still in hot water for running away.

"Some friend you are," Tallack told the dog. Silas tilted his head at him. He did not get it.

"I miss a crowded house. Do you?"

Delores wanted to hear Tallack say yes and so he said yes.

"What I miss are everyday things," Tallack said, "good morning, what's the weather for tomorrow, where's the checkbook, what should we make for dinner? I miss the dailiness, you know? In memory everything is picture perfect, isn't it?"

"Neat as a pin." Which is a fine expression.

"In memory," Tallack told her, "the kids never squabbled about anything. Marie was never grouchy. We recall like that. With holes in it." The Scotch was already going to his head. When Tallack drank he felt a sympathy for humanity that he did not always have.

"I can't imagine Marie ever being grouchy."

"She was like anybody else. Seldom touchy, you know, but grouchy once in a while. If you see the difference."

"When was Marie grouchy?" Delores did not really want particulars. She just wanted conversation.

"Not often, but sometimes. Occasionally the kids used to wear her out."

"Nothing ever seemed to ruffle her."

"I did."

"Pardon?"

"We all have our moments."

"What does 'ruffled' mean?" Delores looked at Tallack over the rim of her glass, coquettishly.

"It means a lot of things. I don't know if life turned out the way she dreamed, and once in a while that caught up with her. That's all I mean."

"Here," says Delores, taking Tallack's surprisingly empty glass, "give me that."

Soon there was ice clinking in glasses again, ice popping when whisky was poured on it. Delores returned with another full glass.

"Good God," Tallack said. "Are you trying to take advantage of me?"

"What did you mean when you said things did not turn out the way Marie dreamed? I have a reason for asking. I'm not just being nosey."

"Nothing monumental," Tallack told her, "just that she had some definite ideas. Anyhow," Tallack said after a moment, searching for the thread of where this thought was supposed to go. "I should not have said yes to this drink."

Glass in hand Delores leaned back against the cushions of her couch. She wished to go on having company.

"What disappointed her?"

"Our house, for one thing. After we bought the place Marie made me promise we wouldn't stay here long. And I promised." Tallack took a cigarette from the pack on the coffee table between them. "Do you mind?"

"Do you need to ask?"

Tallack lit the cigarette with the lighter on the table, a lighter big as a shoe. The flame was an inch high. "It's years since I've seen one of these," he said.

Delores took her cigarettes back and lit one for herself. From deep in her lungs she let out a long stream of smoke; that was smoking. Tallack recollected this.

"Smoking can make you feel better," Tallack said. Delores smiled and tapped the ash off the cigarette.

"You could have been a moviestar. Then you would have moved Marie to Hollywood."

"That would have worked out well. I should have done that."

"I read where Helen Darrow testified in Congress about something."

"I saw that too." Tallack sipped. "Coming out of the army

I didn't have an idea in my head about what I'd do. If you had asked me then," he said, "I don't think I'd have told you that what I wanted was having a house and running Guys & Gals and raising three kids. I was not even sure I wanted to be married. When I got home from the service I barely recalled the wedding."

"I wish my Alen had been more like that," Delores said.

"Like what—frustrated?"

"Flexible. He was stubborn about things if he wanted them. And not always nice about it."

They both turned to Alen's picture on the table beside the couch, as if he were a party to this conversation. The picture showed him at about age 50 in an electric-blue suit, a color fashionable in those years, probably the early 1970s. He was buried in that suit. Alen's polyester shroud will last for eternity. Dig him up, dry clean that suit, good as new.

With his high forehead and long sideburns Alen appeared to be all forebrains.

"Where'd you get that?" Tallack asked. "In our photo album we have that same picture. I'm sure we do."

"Marie snapped it for me on Raymond's high-school graduation day. Alen hardly ever got dressed up and I wanted a record of it. Alen liked Marie awfully." This was a fussy way of speaking—a *locution*.

"He's good-looking in that photograph."

Delores unpinned her gray braid from behind her head. She coiled the braid in the palm of her hand like wealth.

"Alen liked Marie."

"For me," Tallack said, "for me the other part of it was that I came home a little in love with someone else—stuck on someone, I guess is the better way to say it. That weighed on my mind." It was the sort of thing you say when you're a little drunk. He could see Delores was charmed by him. Alcohol gave him insights.

"You rake," she laughed. "You don't seem the type."

"Thanks a lot." Tallack pretended to be offended. He was a little.

"How did Marie handle it?"

"I never told her."

"I'm looking at you with fresh interest, Charles. Who was she? You want another drink?" Even Silas had his ears up for this.

"Someone I worked with from the British army. God no."

"At least you were allies."

"I have a memory in my head clear as day of watching her dry her hair one morning. I swear to God it just ruins me when I think of it, still."

Delores exhaled a long plume of smoke into the center of the room. "You fell in love because you saw a woman drying her hair? Gosh."

"You women do not know the things we find beautiful." Tallack was laughing. "You think it's the obvious stuff, having a big bust or like Marie always worried about her weight."

"I'll take your word for it."

"Nothing sordid happened. I was never the sordid type. If I were I might know more."

"You never talked to Marie about this woman?"

"It might have hurt her feelings. Now everyone is safely dead or whatever. It's such a long while ago. It's only something that happened."

"Sounds like more than that." Delores was needling. Tallack did not like it; the memory was important and now he was sorry he showed it.

"I'm afraid there is no more Scotch," she said.

"I'm glad to hear that."

"Bourbon?"

"Nope. I'm losing my taste for whiskey, I think."

"You wouldn't know it." Delores was teasing him, nodding at his empty glass. "I wonder what Marie's big secrets were," she said. Delores rattled the ice melting in her own glass.

"I'm sure she had them. We all do."

"I recall once, " Delores told him, "Marie and I agreed to chaperone a skating party the school put on for the kids. It was a cold day and apropos of nothing while we watched the kids skate I said, 'Wouldn't a trip to the Caribbean be just the thing about now?' Well, it turned out to be a fantasy Marie had almost daily, almost the way a priest says his office. How about that?" Delores added. "Does that qualify as a big secret?"

"I don't follow."

"Marie said she dreamed about going to Italy all the time. Whenever things got too dreary. She said she went there in her mind." Delores tapped the side of her head with her index finger, indicating "mind."

"We never went to Italy. And it is not in the Caribbean. It is in the other one. The Mediterranean."

"Marie did not *really* think about going. She *imagined* going. She had so much practice she slipped into thinking about it easy as pulling a switch, like a swami going into a trance."

Delores sighed that sigh you hear more from women than from men.

"The fun part," she said, oblivious to how little Tallack understood anything of what she was saying, "the fun part is that you were never there, Charles. Marie said you did not like hot weather."

"I don't mind it so much."

"There was a man." Delores looked at him slyly.

"I'll bite."

"No man in particular. It was a long time ago. Just a man. It didn't bother Marie that it was not you."

"I'm glad for her."

"It was a daydream, Charles, an escape hatch. You see? That's why I bring it up, see? Sometimes Marie felt confined by her life the same way you did. At least a little bit she did. Not that she hated it. Don't think that."

"What did she do with him?"

Delores was puzzled by the question.

"Oh," she said. "They went to a restaurant. And the going to Italy. The big thing for her was that there was always plenty of sunshine in the blue Italian sky and the man was wearing a white cardigan. Marie must have stolen scenes from every romantic movie she ever saw. I remember specifically," she added, "that she called the sky *numinous* when I think she meant *luminous*. I always get both of those mixed up."

"What else?"

"Nothing else."

"Tell me honestly," Tallack said after a long look into his empty glass, "if you think Marie was unhappy. It sounds like she talked to you."

"Maybe that story was only about sex."

"You didn't mention sex."

Delores laughed. "Everybody has their secret parts, Charles, especially about that."

"It's amazing how much I don't know."

"I'm sure." Delores lifted her hand to let several bracelets slide down. They were copper for her arthritis. They clanked.

Dreaming is a way of making sense.

Too many women in Tallack's head. Delores, Cynthia Hipsley, Marie, even Helen Darrow. It was going to be difficult sleeping. His thoughts raced.

Beginning in the morning, Tallack told himself, I am swearing off drinking altogether. And for the longest time he did.

Tallack climbed into his bed wondering if by the time she was an old lady Marie ever let go of all those dreams about Italy and romance. Probably not.

In a syrupy sort of doze Tallack lay in the dark. He was with Marie and seeing her and seeing her and then he was over his head in a deep river. This river, bottomless, flowed through a hissing winter. The air was fogged by snowmelt. Through a fog he could see the river's banks were white with a winter's worth of snow. Around the river bend lights of a city throbbed like an aurora.

He was in the dark, choppy water. The water was painfully

cold. The cold made Tallack heavy, sucking him under. He was afraid to make a choice for one bank or the other; either was too far. Marie's brother Edward stood on the water, Jesus-like. Edward, his hands folded behind his back, curious to see what Tallack would do. Then Edward walked away to answer a telephone.

Like a fish breaking Tallack jerked himself up out of the water. Pushing through the surface of sleep he struggled and thrashed in the dark for the receiver.

"Charles? Charles?" It was Delores. "Don't think I'm crazy," she whispered, "but I'm standing at my window looking across the street at your house. Someone's on a chair in front of your window. They may be trying to climb in over your flower box."

Why was Delores telling him about the flower box if Silas was lost again? Shuffling out to the living room, pulling up his trousers as he went, he saw someone at the front window. They were silhouetted in the streetlamp's light. To reach so high, Tallack reflected, a person would need to be tall.

He stood a moment, certain it would make sense if only he could wake up.

Tallack pulled open his front door and stepped out. He put his weight on the two loose bricks of the top step, the ones he meant to fix for so long. They broke loose at once and pitched him forward. In that instant whoever was at the window was startled off balance. The chair on which they stood tipped over and he fell not ten feet from Tallack's head.

Falling on the hard lawn knocked the wind out of them both. Nothing came out of Tallack when he swore.

"If I'm fuckin hurt I'll sue!"

Sonny Barcelona.

Even before Sonny was on his feet two cops were out of their car. In a flash they had him up by the arms. Delores had called the Ilkeston Park police.

Still not fully awake Tallack lay on the frosted ground looking up at the stars. Beautiful, he thought. And, I am shirtless.

One cop, the bigger one, let go of Sonny and came to Tallack's aid.

Delores hustled across the street in her bathrobe, hair pinned up and wearing some kind of grown. You never saw that woman when she was not dressed with distinction. She came at a trot, pulling her robe tight around herself. Silas jogged at her side looking like he was having the most fun of anybody.

Delores and the cop got Tallack up on his feet. Just to stay vertical he needed to lean on them both. His left ankle felt broken. Flamingo-like he held his left foot off the ground.

"Did he hit you?"

"I never touched him!" Sonny turned to the cop holding his arm, beseeching. The cop said, "Be still!"—sharp, like he meant it.

Tallack noticed the blue glow of a television in the Barcelona's house. Someone was awake. The rest of that house was dark.

Delores and the officer helped Tallack into his house. Silas woofed at the big policeman as if he were trying to give his account. It was embarrassing to Tallack to be so undressed in front of Delores and the cop. It was like one of those dreams people have.

"What happened out there?" the cop asked. "Painting something," answering his own question from the pages of his notebook. He made a further note and asked to use Tallack's kitchen telephone.

Silas followed the cop out to the kitchen, tail wagging. The tags on his collar jingled in a chorus with the keys and cuffs and trigger guard on the cop's black belt.

Delores looked at Tallack's ankle.

"Yikes," she observed.

The cop came back looking newly suspicious.

"What's your relationship like with the neighbors next door?"

"Not good, apparently."

"Did you cross this boy or his family in some way?"

"Not that I know."

"And by the way," Delores put in, "that 'boy' is over 30 years old. Write down in your notebook that he's a half-wit." She craned her neck to see that it was done.

The policeman smiled. "You are the wife?"

"I am the neighbor. It was me who called. Tresca," she added for the notebook.

"What were you doing when this happened?"

"Looking out the window."

"Why were you looking out the window at this hour?"

"My dog barked and it woke me." This sounded like a fib but was maybe true.

The policeman asked Tallack if he was prepared to press charges.

"Charges of what?"

"Vandalism, probably."

"Did he break something?"

"It looks like he defaced the front of your house." The cop peered out the front window into the night. "In the morning we'll see better." He closed his notebook and composed his big face.

"Will you be all right?" The cop addressed Delores. Tallack was annoyed by their concern, and mad about twisting his ankle. All he wanted was to be back in bed and deep asleep.

When the police were gone Delores asked if she should stay. She was fishing in the pocket of her bathrobe for cigarettes.

"Do you have a cup of tea in this house?"

"On top of the fridge. Give me one of those, would you?"

We may focus on the wrong thing and never know.

It was after three A.M. when Tallack nodded off, just in the middle of Delores' recap of the night's excitement. He did not finish the tea she fixed. When Tallack woke she was gone. Before leaving she was thoughtful enough to take the teacups to the kitchen and rinse them. They were face down in the dish drainer as Tallack had been face down on his front lawn.

Late morning the next day Tallack sat facing the street in a redwood chair dragged around from the back patio. "Summer chairs," people used to call them. Tallack looked like the last holdout on an evacuated street. His ankle was swollen too big to even lace his shoe.

The front step had a gap in it where the bricks came out. For Tallack the worst of the damage was to Marie's flower box. Sonny made it as far as **NIGE** in his paint job. He had used a red acrylic spray and his letters looked furry, zany, less angry than if he had made them with a brush.

Under the spring sun Tallack was reading a how-to-fix-it book called *Knock On Wood* one of his kids gave him years ago. The book was open to the chapter on masonry.

Tallack was coming face-to-face with how completely unequipped he had always been for home ownership. After nearly 50 years of it he did not know beans about caring for a house much beyond mowing the lawn.

Delores came across the street with Silas. That day she was wearing some sort of harem pants.

"I saw you sitting. What a mess you've got here."

"Sorry to fall asleep on you last night."

"Silas and I napped with you a little. We only went home after I opened my eyes and saw the day was breaking. I felt so depraved slipping across the street at dawn."

Silas picked out the sunniest spot on the lawn. The dog lay in the light, head bowed because he was old. Tallack admired that dog for the way he was able to relax in any circumstance.

"Look at this," he said, pointing at Marie's flower box. "He can't even spell *nigger*."

"How's your ankle?"

"I took aspirin."

"That'll do a lot of good. Police call you?"

"I called them."

"And?"

"My choices boil down to a charge of criminal mischief or a lawsuit of some sort. I said to whoever I spoke with that I didn't see why I needed to bother."

"What did they say to that?"

"He said he didn't blame me."

"That's it?"

"I'm making lunch. Do you think Silas might like to join me? I'm afraid all I can offer you are eggs." Tallack crossed his legs gingerly. Rolling the ankle even a little bit made it sing with pain.

"My real-estate person Charmane says she's bringing someone by this afternoon. I'm going to tidy up and then make myself scarce. What about Christine? Did she come by to apologize for her idiot child?"

"I hopped out to get the paper this morning and saw her leaving for work, but we didn't speak. She's embarrassed, I guess."

"By Sonny?"

"If he were yours wouldn't you be?"

"If he were mine I'd have strangled him in the cradle."

We bite our tongues.

One afternoon about a week later Tallack was feeling upbeat. The weather was warming and his ankle was better. When we are old we worry an injury will go on and on, that it will trip the chain of events that finally gets us.

Tallack worked in the fresh air chipping ancient cement off the two bricks that came out of his step, imagining himself a sculptor, tap-tapping with a hammer and chisel, careful not to crack the bricks. They were heavy; they had the heft of history. On one edge each brick was rubbed down where people worried it with their coming and going. Tallack was putting the unweathered sides face up. He wanted the place where the steps were repaired to show.

A portable radio played while Tallack worked. Here was one old song he heard:

All those good years
Chase the bad ones.
I recall the love alone, dear,
And can't regret,
Can't regret the heart's lessons.

No idea what it meant. Remorse, probably. The best songs are full of remorse; in happiness there must be a lack of complication that is not hummable. A singer crooning about remorse is more believable than somebody belting out a lyric about soaring hearts aflame. That kind of tune sounds intrinsically insincere, and not very adult.

When no one was around Tallack liked singing.

Cleaning the bricks and mixing the patching cement engrossed Tallack in the pleasure of physical labor, consciously enough to turn the word over in his mind and wonder about its origin: *engross*. He bought a new trowel for this job, a shiny thing looking like it was made for the laying of a cornerstone—ceremonial, you know?

Tallack's attempt to fix his steps by following the instructions in *Knock On Wood* was a failure; it was a useless book, Tallack thought he should leave instructions to burn it when he died.

The cement he mixed set to a sandy consistency and would not hold anything. After letting the bricks dry for a full day Tallack tried putting his weight on them, and they came right out. Hoping to get some advice he telephoned Mitchell Gascogne, the only trained mason he knew or to his knowledge had ever met.

"I read what happened," said Mitchell. "My mother said that was you."

"What do you mean?"

"It was in *The Record*."

"Bad news travels fast. I'm not calling about that."

"My mother was upset."

"Tell her don't be. My neighbors are idiots. Let me ask you a question about masonry."

"Shoot." Mitchell listened and remarked that he did not like the brand of cement Tallack was using; he had a craftsman's disdain for an inadequate tool, and Tallack liked him for that. Mitchell offered to come over to the house and help.

"There's nothing happening for me right now," he said.

"I thought you were apprenticing."

"Yeah, I am, but I haven't landed a full-time gig yet. Let me help you." To which Tallack said no profusely. He would want to pay Mitchell, and Tallack did not know what the charge would be or if he could afford whatever it was. For another larger thing the circumstances would have shamed him. He should have known how to fix his own doorstep.

Later Tallack worried that Mitchell took it all the wrong way, as if what he was really saying was that having Mitchell come around might cause further trouble with the neighbors. If that is what he thought Tallack could not blame him.

"Say hello to your mother. And your father," Tallack added for good measure, as if Mitchell's old man and Tallack were pals.

"Will do," Mitchell said.

Tallack never fixed those steps. For the rest of the years he lived in that house he just walked around the empty space when he came out of his front door. Someone could have broken their neck and sued him for all he was worth, which was not much.

Among the virtues forgiveness is overdone.

Red you want to see.

One day weeks later Johnny phoned from the teacher's room at his school wanting to know if Tallack had time to look after Eileen.

"It happens that I have some hours available. What's your trouble?" Assuming there was trouble.

"No trouble, but you know Terry—from the daycare?

"Sure."

"Terry's getting her divorce finalized so she declared a daycare holiday. Shelly needs to take Abbie to the doctor and she'll be gone all morning."

When Marie was alive they often looked after Eileen if her babysitter failed to show. The sitter was a nice woman but not entirely dependable; she had children of her own and things came up with them. Suspiciously often this happened on a Friday, which was the Tallacks' day for the Home Visitors. He would take Eileen along. Eileen enjoyed the driving around, enjoyed the variety of human nature, like the blind man who whistled and the disturbed young woman who lived in the barn. Even at that age Eileen was not a girl to be put off by strange characters. She sensed that the blind man was harmless and wanted to be taken for comical.

Eileen asked Tallack if they would see the girl in the barn. Marie did not used to like Eileen going into that barn but if Tallack made Eileen stay behind she cried. She called the girl in the barn the Sorry Girl because of the way the young woman continually murmured "I'm sorry" while he went about the business of delivering lunch and collecting the previous day's trays. Ask for her signature on the hospital invoice and she would say "I'm sorry" as she signed it. Eileen did not notice the sad stale stink of socks in the barn because she had never seen anything like the Sorry Girl. Everyone in Eileen's universe connived to create a world in which bears told jokes, flowers sang songs and no one went nuts—how could she not find the Sorry Girl amazing?

"The Sorry Girl got sick and went to another place to stay, honey. And the blind man moved away." To the Big House.

"Holy moly," Eileen replied, as if to say, Gee, the way life slips along.

At Mrs. Posner's house she stopped to admire a clutch of violets by the front path. The flowers made a place to live in the cleft of a limestone slab that somehow split itself.

"Look, Papa. Flowers out of a rock."

"Says a lot about the tenacity of life, doesn't it?"

"Yeah."

Mrs. Posner opened the door, ready to complain that Tallack was late. Her expression dissolved when she looked down and saw the little girl.

"We brought your lunch, Mrs. Posner." Tallack held up the trays to prove it. Eileen scooted under his arms into the house and came up in the middle of the small front room to look around at Derwent Posner's paint-by-numbers menagerie.

"I remember these," Eileen said.

"Do you know that animal above the television?"

"That is a goat."

"How do you know?"

"Because he has a beard."

"My husband had a beard. He liked a goat for that?"

"Maybe." Eileen was willing to concede that such things happen.

For Eileen's lunch Tallack promised to make egg salad. Coming down Buttonwood Street he was surprised to see Christine's blue Volvo parked at the curb in the middle of the day. Christine herself, dolled up in a bottle-green suit, stood at the foot of the driveway, arms folded. She was talking to Sonny, who bounced a basketball. Judging from her look of exasperation Christine was saying something on the order of, "I'm not going to argue anymore." Sonny went on bouncing his ball and taking shots.

Seeing Tallack arrive home Christine tottered up the brick path in her heels and into the house. Sonny stayed where he was taking jump shots. He did not have much of a touch. With all the hours he spent shooting baskets anyone would think he would be better at it.

Sonny took a rebound and looked over at Tallack getting out of his car. Sonny smiled, the dim-witted smile of a juvenile offender. A man of 30, at least. Sonny wound himself in half before slamming the basketball on the driveway. He grinned, pleased with himself, and let the ball roll away. He followed his mother inside. He left the basketball to bounce the length of the driveway. It wedged beneath the front wheel of Christine's Volvo.

Tallack walked to the curb to bring in his empty trash barrel. Even before picking it up he saw the heavy plastic—heavy like the plastic in hospital trays—cut almost in half down one side.

Because of the graffiti on Tallack's flower box Delores had a harder job selling her house. That was her realtor Charmane's theory. Delores did not mention anything about it, though, but once, on Easter Sunday.

Tallack had been to church the evening before with Dennis and Diane; in church he prayed to St. Anthony for their mislaid fertility. Easter was early that year and the morning was chilly. The sun was out.

Tallack was digging in the dirt beneath the window of what had been Maureen's bedroom growing up. In that same spot Marie used to plant peonies. They did well and Tallack wanted to keep them going.

Delores arrived home from church and came across the street to wish Tallack a happy Easter.

"You look pretty," he told her. Tallack wiped his dirty hands on the front of his trousers like a farmer.

"Today's Easter. A girl dresses up." Delores wore a loose-fitting strawberry dress for church with shoes to match. She had a wildly striped scarf slung over one shoulder; Delores never forgot the gypsy touch. The way she looked made Tallack feel more like a bum than usual in work clothes, holes at the knees.

"How does your garden grow?" Delores asked him.

"Like crazy. Everything's coming at once." From all the way across the street Tallack heard Silas bark his wild longing for Delores. "Even the stuff in the flower box is back to life. I haven't done a thing to encourage them."

"I see that."

"What do you think? About the mess?"

Delores pretended an equipoise; Tallack heard that word in his head while she considered her reply. It is a word he felt he ought to use more often for the associations with tranquility that it gave him. As well as associations with horses for some reason. "Equipoise."

"You're not going to leave it up forever, are you? It's pretty raw."

"For a little while I'll be pigheaded. I'll be like whatshisname. Mahatma Ghandi."

"Well, then." Looking at Delores in her strawberry dress Tallack's appetite for revenge was draining.

"Today's Easter. I'm expected to forgive people their trespasses. I'll paint it this week. What do you think of plain white?"

"Too symbolic. Make it something more assertive. Peach. Red geraniums would look good against peach. They would pop. Red you want to see."

In isolation we eat our soul.

Tallack would do this: pop the television on. A ballplayer talked. A pale woman cried. A bearded man explained that all art is about difference. Richard Nixon. Shriveled grandma in a headscarf, in tears. Helen Darrow in a railroad berth. Sports, so many sports. Scenes of arson. Game shows. Two women agreeing about men. Sea otters. Laughter when a fat man did a double take. Soup commercial, everybody said yum. Car chase, shoot-out. Fires, floods, everything but locusts. Cowboys. French movie. Water-skiing.

Locusts.

In the first warm evenings of summer Tallack took to sitting out on his front steps smoking and feeling lonely, which was not altogether unpleasant.

"This isn't the way I envisioned my sunset years," he told Delores one afternoon when she telephoned from Massachusetts to ask if there was any communication from Charmane in the pile of mail Tallack was saving for her.

"Maybe I'm a lunatic." A thought that crossed Tallack's mind more and more. Spending so much of every day alone, nursing his imaginings, Tallack worried he was losing his grip on what small perspective he retained.

Solitude is no good.

Those days Tallack did not miss, not subsequently.

Time leapt ahead. In his solitude Tallack was made dizzy by time.

Late on a sticky August night Tallack was alone in the house when the telephone rang. It rang loud in the all-day quiet to which Tallack was by then accustomed.

A man's voice on the other end of the line asked for someone named Vic.

"Who?" said Tallack.

"Vic."

"You've got the wrong number."

"What number is this?"

"What number are you calling?"

"Is Vic there?"

"There's no one here named Vic."

"What's your name?"

"Vic."

"Listen, Vic. Would you like to meet new people?"

No, Tallack would not.

We catch ourselves envying the dead their rest.

The first couple of years following Marie's death Tallack carried forward on the old momentum. Life was unpleasant with the people next door but Tallack's theory was that the tension kept him fit.

Across the street he still had Delores. They spoke every day or nearly; she was a great friend to make so late in life. Now and again she disappeared up to her son Donny's house in Massachusetts for a week or two. Then Tallack would miss her like mad. She never said so but Tallack knew Delores went there to dry out.

There was an afternoon when Tallack met her out walking Silas. She asked him in for tea. This was immediately a proceeding of tumblers and ice cubes. I'll pass, he said. He preferred the tea.

"Not even a little?" The way drinkers do, Delores wanted a partner.

"Lately I haven't got the taste for it."

"You don't miss it?"

"I don't think so." Growing old Tallack lost most of his desire for alcohol. It felt less like he gave up on drinking and more like drinking gave up on him. For Delores the opposite appeared to be true.

Not long after this Silas died. Within a month of the dog's death Delores told Tallack she was leaving, goodbye, and going to live with the son. A thrill went through Tallack, not the sweet kind.

"It is the end for us, Charles."

"I've heard you sing that song before."

"Darling, it is true. Donny's insisting, and now Silas is gone I've got no excuse. No rationale."

"Twelve months from today we'll be having this same conversation." Tallack was wrong. Within weeks Delores found a buyer willing to pay what he thought a fantastic amount for her house.

Before the movers came Delores and Tallack behaved like lovers bracing for the inevitable end, like Tallack and Cynthia did 50 years before. All their moments together were wound tight, seeing each other every day for a cigarette, for drinks if that was what Delores wanted, full of affection they said out loud, on edge all the time. All that mush.

Tallack thought seriously of asking Delores to marry him, assuming she would have him. What a turn of events that would have been. Tallack was clear-headed about how much work she would be, with the booze. More than anything, at the end of the day age and loneliness could not change Tallack's tie to Marie, always to Marie, largely.

Delores moved to Massachusetts. At first Tallack spoke with her several times a month. It was awkward for him. He always felt in need of a pretext for ringing. If the son Donny picked up Tallack was suddenly bashful as a teenager.

"Feels like I'm asking your old man if Delores can come to the phone," he told Delores once. Tallack could tell she was pleased by that; he guessed she had not flirted for a long time. He ached for her company.

After Sonny Barcelona died of a burst aneurism in his brain Tallack phoned her, and then again three days later after Sonny's funeral at the church to tell her about that.

"You went? I thought you would not."

"I didn't want to be petty. If I felt anything I felt sorry for the life he had."

"You were well brought up, Charles."

"I am a prince."

"Did you speak to Christine?"

"I didn't speak to anybody."

Tallack phoned Delores after Maureen was diagnosed. A year or so after her marriage ended Maureen told him it was doctor's orders that she needed to move in with this fellow she had been seeing—Jay—because she had begun having problems with her legs. For years she had had funny feelings in them but it was always coming and going. No one ever concluded anything from it; Tallack just thought she was not graceful in, whatever, dancing. Then, all of a sudden, or so it felt to Tallack, Maureen's problems were more coming than going. Her doctor said she was not supposed to be alone.

"And who's the fellow you mentioned?" asked Delores

when Tallack told her about Maureen.

"She has got this thing called *LOMS*, which every time I say it reminds me of that actor—remember him?"

"What do you do for that?"

"'Late onset multiple scleroses.' Saying 'LOMS' is less impolite than just saying 'multiple sclerosis'. Maureen insists it's fine but she is supposed to keep an eye on it. So she moved in with this guy. That way *he* can keep an eye on it."

"Are her boys around?" Manny and Mo.

"No, no, she tells me it is not that sort of a thing."

"What sort of thing?"

"She doesn't want me making a big deal out of it. I told her I never make a big deal."

"Which is false."

"Says you."

"Can she walk?"

"Well enough. Dennis and I flew down to see her for a few days last week and she met us at the airport. She was in a wheelchair because her hips hurt that day. I'm telling you, Delores, I could have cried to see her in that goddam thing. But she was all right. She can get up on these steel crutches she has. I hate the sight of them."

"What do you make of the 'friend'?"

"Who's that? Jay?"

"Who else are we talking about?"

"Decent guy. I keep thinking why didn't she marry this one instead of the dentist." With his tootsies.

"Life might not have turned out any differently for her, Charles. You never know."

"Sometimes you know."

"You think it is serious?"

"With Jay or the illness?"

"Pick."

"It's not a love match. Don't get the wrong idea. Jay was married to a friend of hers, Roberta or something, then the friend died. My sense talking to him is that Jay misses being married and taking care of someone. The requirements of it, however you call it, the obligations are a pleasure to him. That is my sense."

"I've met the type."

By the end of Delores' first year up in Massachusetts there was more space between their phone calls. Then early in the second winter Donny phoned to say Delores died.

"She passed away in the doctor's arms," said Donny. "She went in for a stress test."

"I guess she failed," Tallack said to Donny. That same afternoon he lost his keys and needed to have a new set made.

Tallack was losing his attachment not to this earth but to time, which is to say he felt antagonism toward its passing. Time snuck off with his loves, his strength, his goddam keys.

Thus my declining years, Tallack told himself.

When it was Delores' turn to die and join everybody in paradise Tallack's first impulse was to be envious. She was finally through the gate, done with this life and up there in the bright clouds. The at last.

On to redemption, Tallack thought. He thought this although he knew everything about it was baloney.

Around this same time Helen Darrow moved to heaven as well. Helen was 74 when she died. She had not made a movie in seven years. Her last role was as someone's granny in *Rage of All Nations,* a World War II extravaganza that came and went. Helen was never seen in public again except for a single year when she handed out an Oscar for something or other.

Helen and her daughter owned property in Oregon on which they built a refuge for orphaned zoo animals. The animals were the daughter's interest. (Helen's obituary hinted that the daughter had personal troubles at some point in her past.) The daughter kept a leopard in the house, and one day the leopard turned on Helen. It was a bad reason to be back in the headlines.

Worse, Helen's ending was the sort of ghoulish finish for an old movie star that she would have described as soap opera. Awful to think the manner of Helen's death will be what she is remembered for, what people will talk about when her movies are shown.

Meanness, gossip are part of this world; no one needed to tell Tallack. It discouraged him to know it, still.

In his very old age Tallack had steadily less patience with philosophy, and he had never had much.

Thanks to the women in his life Tallack was always tied to this earth and to this life. Women sustained his yearning for this world over the next one (even if the next one is where all the pretty girls in his life had gone, but for Cynthia). Tallack's womanlessness was something he pretended was only a phase he was going through, like an illness of which he would eventually be cured. He wanted more life, more pretty girls, his strength back, more.

Tallack was tired. And still he had no interest in leaving this earth. But he was about to do exactly that.

Returning memories?
No, at the time of death
I'd like to see lost objects
return instead.

Avalanches of gloves,
coats, suitcases, umbrellas—
come, and I'll say at last:
What good's all this?

Wisława Szymborska
"Still Life With a Balloon"

A life is an endless interlocking.

Tallack's last six months were crowded. It was 2010. Tallack was 86.

How long did Tallack live with Dennis—two years, three years? It was after Delores died, he knew that. Dennis had been promoting the idea from the day Marie died. Like anyone else Tallack wanted to stay in his own home. More than that Tallack thought he wanted to be left alone. All his life he pictured himself as a character who throve on solitude, if he could only just get some. He was wrong in his self-perception. Until he was widowed Tallack never guessed how entire loneliness could be. A dark thought would settle on him and stay there for days. This was the effect of isolation.

It took time but Tallack finally worked out that solitude was an unfurnished place that would have killed him slowly, miserably.

And then Eileen was pregnant. That is how it felt to Tallack: And then Eileen was pregnant.

Like her own conception Eileen with a baby coming was quite a big surprise. She was 22, older than Tallack's mother was when she gave birth to him. Eileen was in college—who expects this from a college girl in these days?

Tallack was at Johnny and Shelly's house in Ilkeston on a Sunday. Dennis and Diane were there. Eileen had been home on her Christmas break from her college in Delaware. Johnny was passing around stemmed glasses of wine and wow was he mad at Eileen.

"She mentions this on the morning she's going back to school. Literally when we're pulling into the airport lot."

"Do you know the boy? The father?" asked Diane in that way she had of going slightly ahead of the conversation sometimes with her questions.

"What burns my ass," Johnny not answering, "is that I'm not sure how well *Eileen* knows the father."

"I thought you were going to wait for me before you told them," Shelly said when she came into the kitchen. Her remark was a poke at him. Their marriage had come to that kind of place.

At this time Johnny and Shelly no longer appeared to like each other. Steadily they let something get started between them, they nursed some sour thing. Tallack laid it all at Johnny's feet. Fifty-seven years old and Johnny still felt to his father like an unformed man. Shelly had enough of him; she was 59 by then. Tallack thought it was bad for their girls to witness, Eileen and Abbie, bad for the picture it gave them of marriage and married people.

"I *was* waiting for you," Johnny protested to Shelly.

Back to that. Shelly had been elsewhere in the house helping Abbie finish a homework project—a family tree tracing names and begats on a kind of ivy vine. Abbie was pleased with herself for thinking to draw a picture of a closed-up leaf bud as a way of holding a place for the baby in her sister's womb. It was this project that would lead to where Tallack was months later, contemplating his end, the actual thing.

"What month is she in?" Diane asked because now she had hold of it.

"Third."

"She is going to *have* the baby?"

"Looks like. She's 22. We no longer get a vote."

Just to point out, much of what Tallack heard of this conversation came in less through his ears than through the surface of his skin; he was getting to be exactly that deaf, especially in a crowd. Tallack was aware of his bad hearing; it was not news to him. So his reaction to what Johnny was telling them was less about Eileen than about taking the big perspective.

Tallack foresaw that Eileen would have at first a complicated time of it and then everything would work itself out, more or less, which Tallack did not need to tell himself is the best anyone gets. Eileen would be fine as anybody.

Naturally Tallack was thinking about the night Johnny introduced him to Shelly and mentioned by the way that *she* was pregnant. So the tone Johnny was using when he talked about Eileen bothered Tallack quite a lot; later he wished he had spoken up. Some good might have come of it and everyone might have been better in the long term.

"You wouldn't think he's had two weeks to gain perspective

on this, would you?" Shelly said.

"She never *thinks*."

"Who never thinks—me?" Shelly volleyed with that.

"Your daughter."

"So this would be more like her fourth month?" said Diane.

"You were sitting there doing the math, Diane," said Johnny. "I knew you would." Out the corner of Tallack's eye he saw Dennis sit up straighter and Shelly too. "I'm teasing," Johnny said. "Don't take me so serious."

"Were you surprised?" Diane turned her attention now to Shelly. Tallack was getting the edgy feeling they all got around Diane.

"I'm not thrilled about it," Shelly told her, "and I wish it was not so. But when you're that age it happens."

"Not to me it didn't," Johnny answered. "Not to Dennis. Not to Diane."

So there, that did it. Now Diane was sad because she had not gotten knocked up as a college girl.

"Not to you, Pop?" said Shelly. Nice save, Shelly.

"To be fair there was a war on," Tallack said. Shelly was a good woman, and Tallack thought he would like her in the next life as well as he had liked her in this one, if that turned out to be a possibility.

Then Abbie walked in. The conversation shifted to her swimming team and schoolwork and so on.

No one spoke for the first few minutes of the ride home. Until the heater came around it was cold in the car. The cold was a shock to Tallack's heart. That woke him up. After a second of silence Diane said, "That wasn't much fun."

"No," Dennis answered. He was being careful not to give his wife a stepping off point for a full review or else she would go on and on.

Tallack was still not used to back seats, to not being the driver. He found it hard to stay attached to conversations from there. His deafness did not help. He was staring at the back of Dennis' head and its little bare patch. Feeling affection for the back of his boy's balding head Tallack's eyes welled a little. When he got old he noticed that he sometimes cried unexplainably. It annoyed him, honestly it did. Tallack still had all his hair. Pattern baldness is inherited from the mother's line.

"Give her a break, Diane," Dennis said. "It's hard to be 22 years old. Or do you forget?" They were both over 60, on the front porch of becoming old.

Dennis spoke in a good-humored way. Tallack knew that Diane, hunched behind the wheel in an overwhelming wool coat, was aggravated with Dennis because he mentioned the youth which she had no longer. That far Tallack had her figured out.

Tallack asked himself Dennis' question—what could he recall of being 22? Tallack was a man of 86 years old. In his mind stray bits of old time were always floating loose, like the plaque in his arteries. Himself by the radio reading a book while his mother turned the pages of a newspaper, neither one of them speaking, just the two of them at home. A pretty girl he saw in a red hat waiting at a corner for the light to change just after he came back to New York from the war; Tallack knew the corner still, he could have gone there right that minute. The pretty girl would be gone, gone from the corner anyhow, gone a long time from this earth most likely.

What Dennis was asking in his question was the way it felt to be filled up with want, want beyond description and for that reason attaching itself to every single thing that comes along. Want so big it gave a glimpse of imminence.

It is good to want like that. Old people forget this.

Desires rule us.

It was the tired end of winter when they all learned about Eileen. Two months later the days remained chilly but were brighter and thank God longer; it was possible to believe life would come back.

Like a hibernating bear Tallack emerged from the house just to feel the sun on his face, just to look up into it and let it beam upon him. Sunlight was like food to him.

On one of those warm days Tallack walked with nothing in mind to the bottom of the block. Down the corner there was a Presbyterian church. The church was distinctive for its stone turret, above which flew what Tallack assumed was the Presbyterian pennant, blue and red. He meant to find out what the colors meant but he never did.

Soon he was going into the church a couple of times a week. There were no steps to climb, which given Tallack's old legs was the most welcoming thing about the place. And no one shooed him out.

The sanctuary smelled of the stone that made the walls and of smoke and of old cloth, the smells of church inside. Down the length of every pew were laid red runners, worn shiny from all those Presbyterian backsides. Tallack could never resist running his hand over them (the runners).

One day just as Tallack sat down a small White woman, handsome in her middle age, crossed the transept. Her hard leather heels echoed sharp on the stone floor. Against her hip she beat a file folder; she was in a hurry. She wore a grey tweed skirt. Spotting Tallack in a pew she waved her file folder at him and he waved back. After that he saw that woman almost every visit. She never asked what he was doing in her church. She must have thought Tallack was giving Presbyterianism a good long look.

The thing to which Tallack was giving a long look was the hair on that woman's head, wild hair, salt-and-pepper *acerbic* hair she fought back with a red clip. The red clip in her graying, sprung hair—man, the effect of that on Tallack was great.

Tallack understood that when this woman looked at him she saw a feeble old boy, old old old. If you are old old old you are so invisible most of the time usually no one notices you staring. Tallack simply had the largest respect for that woman's hair. It was hair like Cynthia Hipsley's once was, not in its color but in the way it was beyond subjugation.

Women still stimulated Tallack's nerve endings. That never went away even as he piled up years. He remained greedy for this life. He was not giving up.

Think about this: Tallack's favorite photograph of Marie, the one which fixed time at a single moment, was the snapshot he kept in a frame on the table next to his bed at Dennis and Diane's house. It was beside him like an aid to meditation. It was taken at a New Year's party. On the wall behind Marie there are cardboard numbers taped "1955," probably the year that was coming rather than the one that was ending; presumably that was the tradition, Tallack never thought about it. People in the photograph wear paper hats. Where they were nor anything else about the party Tallack could not call to mind. Just the same there was himself on a folding chair in the foreground, gesturing with a cigarette in his hand to someone outside the frame of the photo. Tallack looks animated about something, God knows what.

Marie and Barbara Riordan are the focus of the photographer's interest, not Tallack, and no wonder. They are barely 30. At the end of a sofa, oblivious to the picture taker, or pretending to be. Barbara with a highball gripped in both hands and a paper napkin spread across her lap. Marie young enough to want to look good on New Year's Eve, and she does. Her eyes focus on some point to her left, over Barbara's shoulder. She is positively glamorous in a shiny dress with a sweetheart neck, Barbara's with a high collar. Marie wears fake pearls (which Tallack knew were fake because he bought them) and in her hands in her lap is a cigarette between two fingers of her right hand. Until people started worrying about it so much Marie liked a cigarette as much as he did. Tallack forgot that.

In the photograph Tallack saw the pretty girl who caught his eye the first day he met her. He loved how her hair fell forward and the way her bright eyes peaked out, half hidden. By New Year's Eve 1955 Marie was beginning to get a grown woman's more interesting look; the features of her face hint at women's knowledge. Her features were definite, not like a girl's.

If ever Tallack talked about her body Marie did not like it. She considered herself always on the verge of being fat. Really it was only in the last ten years of life that Marie put on weight. Tallack never noticed except she was always pointing it out.

The camera never lies, they say.

Some place Tallack had another snapshot of himself in Army days, somewhere in the Kentish countryside with Syd Ballard and Cynthia Hipsley. They stand in front of a truck, a white five-pointed star on its door. They are grimacing, razzing whoever holds the camera. The sun is shining from the left; it appears to be early evening. Wow are they young.

Shortly before he died Cynthia sent Tallack a newer picture, herself surrounded by grown-up grandchildren. She is at the center of this picture in some shapeless smock with cabbage roses on it, some nightgown sort of a thing, Cynthia old old old like Tallack. Her smile is the same but her copper-colored hair is all gone. She wears her hair in a stubble of white. The annihilation of Cynthia's hair was an offense, an indignity. Tallack tore the photograph up and afterward tried to flush its memory from his mind.

Here is part of what Cynthia's letter said:

> *Charles, two mornings ago I was alone here when the wonderful thing happened for the first time in ever so long. It was much too wet to put my head out of doors and so I watched some cookery show on the television, feeling quite sorry for myself. (You might know this*

feeling but I hope you do not!) Altogether blue I opted for my bed, hoping a sleep might erase my mood. Thinking about this and that as I drifted off. That was when the <u>*thing*</u> *flooded me—floored me, really, a feeling like taking on extra weight and being dizzy with the exertion. It was so wonderful—the great* <u>*warmth*</u> *of it—that I feared my time had come. The thought occurred that some other woman was right that minute looking for this sensation but that by mistake it had been delivered to me. All quite mystical really.*

I felt it strongly that I must let you know that this still sometimes happens to me.

Tallack knew just what she meant but not for certain. "Gnomic" was not a word he would use. But for Cynthia he was thinking it.

Down at the Presbyterians the day aged and went grey.

Most of us are capable of compassion.

One afternoon that April, a bit past four o'clock, Tallack came in from the Presbyterians to find Diane home early from her job. She was sitting on the couch with a small book open on her lap.

"I left work early to see the doctor," she said. That sounded deliberately allusive, as though Diane expected a follow-up question. Tallack gave in.

"You're all right?"

"Female thing. Wholly routine."

"You look worn."

"I am a little, yeah."

"Make you a cup of tea?"

"No thanks, Pop. Where were you? I was half beginning to get worried."

"Down at that church."

"Really? And here I was praying. We should have joined forces to storm heaven."

"Must be the Holy Hour." It was not even 4.30. "Need anything?"

"No. Just praying."

"I meant the tea or something like that." He would have liked tea.

It was dark in the room, and cold, and Tallack was thinking, How can she just sit in the gloom?

Tallack had no doubt Diane was praying. Two or three years before she went to the wedding of a friend's daughter in a full-gospel church. All those people waving their arms around like palm fronds got to her. "Great theater," she said, too cerebral to admit she was thrilled. "I can't conceive any Jesus, but I am moved by their belief." Now she was going to that church for half the day every Sunday. Tallack could not follow her logic but everyone's faith is their own—one light, many windows, isn't that the saying? If something nourished her then Tallack was glad for Diane. And also it took some of the heat off Dennis. At least he got Sunday mornings off.

"Come sit by me, Pop," Diane said.

"Sure you don't want tea?"

Diane patted the place beside her on the couch. She smiled with her wide eyes. She wore her grey hair close to her head now. The big bosom she had back when she married Dennis was deflated. But still she was dark and pretty—that Sicilian complexion, you know? Dennis once told Tallack that the countermen at the 7-11 always said a big hello to her, thinking that like them Diane might be from Pakistan.

"Once the sun goes down it gets cold," Tallack said. "My hands ache."

"I was on the phone with Shelly a few minutes ago."

"And how is Shelly?"

"Fine. I was thinking about Eileen and I felt I should

offer to help if I could." If Diane was the sort of woman who made broad jokes—if she were *arch*—Tallack would have assumed she was making a wisecrack.

"That was a nice thing to do."

"What the hell did I say to Shelly, do you mean?" Somewhere in Diane was a sense of humor. Credit for that.

"Yes."

"I offered to introduce her to my friend Theresa whose daughter got *her*self pregnant. I suggested Theresa might know about some resources or have some insight."

Insights into what, thought Tallack, though what came out was, "That could be helpful."

"Shelly said no thank you."

"They need to manage this for themselves."

"Even dialing the number I was asking myself what am I doing this for? Theresa's daughter never speaks to her. God, Pop, I go through life embarrassing myself." And here Diane started to cry and Tallack thought to himself, Oh Christ.

"Why do you say that, honey? You wear yourself out that way."

Ages ago Tallack read in some magazine like *Time* that when a woman cries a man should hold her and say nothing at all until she stops, to just wait her out. That is what Tallack did then, though it required him to stand up and sit down again to get within range of Diane's shoulders, which was not a fluid movement.

Diane wept five minutes at least. Not wracking sobs, you know, but pretty steady.

Tallack held Diane with sincere care. Over her shoulder his eyes fell on the clock that was on the end table behind her. Tallack could not hear its click click but he knew from the stutter of the sweep hand that it must be making that sound.

That clock's case is made of walnut, he reflected, dark like that. And, Never in my life have I pursued comfort but I like this house. It is warm. The rooms are always picked up; every two weeks a woman comes in and does a thorough cleaning. The bathrooms and the kitchen are shining and clean. There is the big TV over there that none of us watch. People speak quietly. It is like living in a shop where nice things are sold.

Diane stopped crying. She coughed lightly, like a swimmer surfacing, and only continued to rest against Tallack from some sort of inertia. She seemed OK.

Late afternoon is a good time to have company, the sun setting out there, a cozy chill creeping through the house. It is not good to be alone at that hour.

On the windowsill was a shivering geranium that was managing to bloom out of season. Keeping it alive through that winter was one of Diane's projects. She thought she could breed for hardiness. Tallack looked at that plant thinking "etiolated," not sure if that was the word he wanted. That geranium was pallid.

Tallack knew the stillness was coming for him. Or just deeper deafness, or only the day closing in.

Tallack was falling asleep. He was half dreaming of a big white house off isolated by itself. He did not know the house but it appeared that he lived in it. His mother and Marie sat at a table beside each other. They shared a deck of photographs and shuffled through them one by one, talking over each other. His mother held up one of the photographs and said mean things about the man in it. Tallack stood at her shoulder, straining to get a look at the picture. Marie said something teasing about minding manners but his mother went on and on about the man in the photograph, like someone past caring about being mean.

Out the window beside this dream house a plowed field was sugar-dusted in snow. Tallack felt the cold on it. In sleep his finger bones ached.

We divine,
we glimpse,
we sense.

Eileen came home after she graduated college on Mother's Day in 2010. Johnny and Shelly did not make a big fuss of the event.

A few weeks later in June Eileen introduced Tallack to the father of her baby—"the boy," Johnny called him—Del, which Eileen told her Tallack was short for Delassandro. That was his surname, Tallack assumed; until afterward the question did not occur to him. Eileen was dropping Del at the airport when she brought him by to see Tallack.

Tallack was sitting in the front yard of the Dennis and Diane house. At some point in the past Diane put wrought-iron chairs under the willow tree that was out there—for the charm—and in one of them Tallack sat half dozing in the sun. He was considering whether to make lunch or take a walk down to the Presbyterians when Eileen pulled up to the curb.

She was out of the car before Tallack even recognized her—did she register that he could not place her face right away? It was not only that he had been half napping. She waddled with pregnancy and her face had turned broad with the gaining weight. She looked almost matronly when in Tallack's eyes she was supposed to be still a kid.

The boy Tallack did not completely take in at first, distracted as he was by the word *paranormal*, which trotted across his brain when he heard—he swore he heard—when he heard Marie's voice saying, "*He* doesn't look like much." If it was really Marie talking she was right. Walking toward Tallack across the front lawn the boy stooped like a person skulking. It was not because he was tall either.

"I didn't think I'd be seeing you," Tallack said, or something to that effect. He pushed himself up from the iron chair. It was important for Tallack to meet his granddaughter on his feet.

"I wanted you to see Del."

"I see Del. How are you, Del?"

Del's shoulders were too broad for his head; the disproportion brought to mind a cartoon turtle the kids used to watch on the TV. Like Eileen's friend the turtle had what people used to call a "sleepy eye," which made him look up and sideways, like he was afraid of being struck from the side. Tallack went to grade school with a kid—his name was Philip Turner—who had one of his eyes that way.

A wind blew. Abruptly the day was cold and they headed indoors.

"We can't stay long." Eileen did not want Tallack getting any hopes.

"There's more than two hours," the boy Del said.

"And you have to check in one hour before." Sad hearing the pair of them speak that way, in the manner of people married too long. Too bad for the boy, of course, but all Tallack cared about was Eileen.

"I need to go to the bathroom bad. Do you mind, sir?"

"First door you come to on the north."

"The north?"

"The right."

"Don't dawdle," Eileen called after.

"I will not because that would be rude."

Once the boy was gone Tallack could smile—he could beam—at his darling granddaughter.

"Del is louche," Eileen remarked.

"I'm sure he's just tired. He'll grow into the role of father. Most of us do. The majority. Tell me how you met."

"We didn't 'meet.' Papa, I'm not marrying him."

"I am consumed with relief."

Eileen had not asked for his approval. Tallack's bluntness was a consequence of being what he said: consumed with relief. Eileen laughed out loud and the sun broke through, the actual sun, it flooded the room with middle-of-the-day white light.

"If I can ask, why did you bring Del home to your parents? I'm sure nobody enjoyed it, least of all him."

"Because now I never have to do it again."

"That is astute, honey. You're a smart girl."

"I'm subtle. When the summer term is over Del's going in the army."

"The army? Will they take him with a baby?"

"I'm having the baby, Papa."

"Of course."

"He's already enlisted. It's in his family's tradition for the men."

"And then what?"

"After the baby?"

"Ever."

"I will not erase him from the kid's life. I'm being hard with him now just to make things clear. I'm not mean but Del'd be a disaster. I have drawn that conclusion." Eileen did not trouble to lower her voice. "At least I'll get the child support from the army. Or so I'm told."

Tallack admired Eileen's hard-heartedness toward Del. Hard-heartedness is an underrated quality, which Tallack came to discover in his last innings.

Tallack was sitting again and Eileen was still standing over him so that her bump could not be ignored.

"How is your baby?"

"Better and better. It is ripening apace, or like a peach. Is that the expression?"

"Your doctor is happy?"

"Thrilled to pieces."

"You'll be a good mother."

"I don't know anything about it."

"Life is for learning."

"You sound like a fortune cookie, Papa. The thing's moving—want a feel?"

Eileen lifted her grandfather's hand to her belly and the kid kicked him square in the meaty part of his thumb—could Tallack ever forget that? No, he could never. Tallack looked up at Eileen, delighted.

"It said hello."

"Pretty cool, right?" Del came back from the bathroom fluttering his hands to dry them. "I don't ever get over it." And Tallack thought, *You* touch my granddaughter's belly?

"Don't get everybody wet."

"I did not want to use the clean towels."

The boy told a story meant to be funny, about how when he arrived the previous Sunday he dropped his suitcase in Eileen's bedroom. Johnny was right behind him moving the bag to the living room.

"He tells me the couch is very comfortable," Del said, "and so I answer him, 'It's a little late to be guarding your daughter's virtue.' That's my stupid sense of humor, but when I said it you could cut the ice. He looked like he wanted to kill me."

"Dad *did* want to kill you."

"He'd settle for breaking my legs. It's your mother who wants me dead. She really hates me." It interested Tallack that the boy thought he would enjoy hearing this story. Tallack never wished to be the type of old man young people confided in.

Owing to his deafness their voices came to Tallack from a distance. This experience of conversation—as broken English—made him edgy; he had to work at translating everything using context.

Tallack's head dipped and for a moment he slept, deep enough to dream. There was the image of a black train, blurred but definitely there. It was like stepping away for a moment.

Eileen cleared her throat loud enough to make her grandfather stir.

"Do you need to go already?" How irritating that he drifted off; now she was being kind to him. Goddammit, Tallack despised being a geezer.

When Tallack moved in Dennis assumed an obligation to take him to church, and therefore Tallack felt an obligation to go. Besides he liked being alone with Dennis. Coming and going in the car to the church they talked about ordinary things. Tallack could listen to his son without the anxiety of knowing Dennis needed to keep half an eye on his wife in case something fell upon her ears unhappily.

Tallack liked sitting beside Dennis at Mass in the church whose name he never troubled to learn. That church had hardworking stained-glass windows, he used to think—scenes of horror, visions of wonder.

In church Tallack was always glad that, being deaf, he could not hear the preaching. All his life Tallack felt irritated by sermons—and not only because like the rest of us he did not like to be talked at. It was that most of those guys took so little care with their words, like they could not spare 20 minutes to organize their thoughts about holy scripture. With his deafness Tallack heard only a diffident drone. He found this a real blessing. One evening on the way home from church he happened to express that to Dennis.

"Maybe you should have been a Sufi," Dennis replied. "I think that's how they pray."

"Like how?"

"Against the droning. I think they dance."

From nearly a century of habit and under the influence of the candle-wax smell Tallack never forgot to say a prayer for the repose of Marie's soul. Not that he believed in prayer, in that kind of prayer. What the hell—God needs reminding that we are all still out here, still spinning around in outer space and working on our problems?

At the reading of the gospel that evening Tallack observed a young man three pews up who bore a resemblance to Eileen's friend Del—slight in the same way, and with such poor posture looking like he might actually tip over. His head was likewise too small for his body. That may have been an embellishment supplied by Tallack's imagination. And both of this guy's eyes were open; he did not have the sleepy eye like Del.

This young man was with a girl with an uncertain face, neither pretty nor plain. When it was time to stand the girl leaned into the boy—was she unhappy, was she hungry for anything? What did that girl want?

Everything, she wanted everything.

Hearts ache at the gorgeous light.

Then two weeks went by like nothing at all and the warm spring came at last. Birds sang, the earth greened up, moist smells everywhere you sniffed, the whole business. Everyone's mood lifted.

The school term finished in May and Eileen came home. In spite of themselves her parents were excited about the baby—in spite of Del and all of that. Tallack liked the way Eileen went on deflecting everybody's questions about what she and the child would do next fall.

"One thing at a time," she told them. Awfully cool about it for 22, Tallack thought, and admiringly.

On Memorial Day they were again to Johnny and Shelly's house. Dennis and Tallack came from the church and they met Diane there. Walking into that backyard Tallack had the peculiar sense of stepping onto a movie set, déjà vu drawn from his experience of making *Against All Currents*, probably. It was not yet dusk and the green of late spring saturated the whole scene, trees and all. There was something *pending* in the air that evening, some alteration poised to happen. Pretty as it was the light seemed artificial.

The scene opened on Diane laughing with Johnny. She held a glass of wine by its stem; Tallack knew at a distance they were both a little drunk. With one hand Johnny tended the chicken he was grilling, a sort of skill. With his free hand he had got his fingers wrapped around an icy glass of Scotch. So he would not have far to walk for his next one Johnny had the bottle outdoors with him. It sat on a little table there in the yard.

One house over a dog barked, as if they needed background noise for atmosphere.

Enter Eileen through the back door, big as anything in her last month of pregnancy, so ready to pop she had to step sideways down the steps to greet her Uncle Dennis and her grandfather.

"The elephant enters the room," said her father.

"You're funny, daddy."

"Aunt Maureen wants you to call her."

"I will." Eileen sat and bounced straight back up.

"That chair's puddled," Johnny said.

"For a moment there I thought my water broke." They both knew she would be leaving the family soon, some way. Time was running out on their father-daughter routine. Time was against them.

"Take my chair," Tallack told Eileen. Honestly he preferred to stand. At his age his whole life seemed to occur sitting down.

"How is Maureen?" Dennis poured Tallack a glass of that

pink wine Diane was drinking. The wine was so cold and sweet it ached Tallack's back teeth.

"Shelly talks to her. She's better at understanding Maureen on the phone than me. I feel bad about it but there's nothing I can do."

Diane said, "Nothing wrong with her mind." Typical of Diane she came at a subject from her own special direction. Immediately Dennis became attentive.

"The being sick seems to have plateaued," Johnny remarked.

"Or maybe that we're just all just used to it," said Dennis. "I'm only glad she's not alone. I don't think she ever sees the boys." That would be Maureen's sons, Manny and Moe.

"Which long term will be a blessing," Dennis said. "When they finally go to prison Lou will get stuck for the bail money."

Tallack did not like this flippancy. It was mean, however it was meant.

"Where's Shelly?" he asked.

"Helping Abbie with a school thing."

"Tell Papa what you need, Eileen," said Diane. This time when she interjected Diane shook with little movements of restraint, like she was barely keeping the lid on herself. That woman amazed Tallack. How exhausting to be her.

"There's nothing I need, Aunt Diane. I'm good."

"Your history paper?"

"You're confusing me with Abbie." Diane never connected with Eileen. Eileen had too much undirected energy. She was never Diane's idea of a child.

"I'm not confusing you."

"Abbie!" Johnny shouted up the backsteps. Tallack recalled Marie always scolding her kids for shouting in the house. She used to tell them it was bad behavior.

Abbie appeared with a teenager's elaborate annoyance, all sighs and shrugs. She had been with that computer. Time on that thing made her irritable.

"Hi, Papa." Tallack loved looking at this granddaughter, short and dark like her mother, confidence in her eyes. Tallack thought both his granddaughters were brilliant.

"Ask Papa for your project, Abbie. Use your recorder app." Johnny tipped a little more of that Scotch into his glass, just a taste. This was his impersonation of a man pursuing moderation.

"What's this about?" Tallack asked Eileen.

"She needs to write your biography for school."

"Why me does she need?"

"Of anybody you've got the most amount of material," Eileen told him. "I did you too when I was in high school, if you recall."

"Then why don't you just give her the one you wrote? There haven't been any major updates since."

"If I wanted to I could. I saved what I wrote in a box, which is somewhere. Someday I can read it to my baby."

"Assuming I'm not still around in person to bore the poor kid myself."

Abbie already had the recorder running when she came back with her phone. She pointed it straight at her grandfather like a gunman in a stick-up. In her concentration she knocked against Johnny's elbow, sloshing his drink.

"Careful, love. Don't spill the magic." Tallack knew it was

unkind but he was glad if Johnny's comment was recorded. Tallack hated the kind of thirst his son had. He did not mind that people drank, or even that some *needed* a drink. But Johnny had no need, he only lacked restraint. There is a difference. Tallack had seen it all his life.

"What year were you born, Mr. Tallack?" Abbie asked.

"I was born in 1924."

"How old are you now?"

"Ask yourself what year is this and then you'll know."

"Where were you born?"

"New York City, USA."

"What was your father's name?"

"Dempster. He died before I was born and I don't know his first name. Then my mother married a man named Donald Tallack. But I'm told everyone called him Jack."

"Why?"

"That is a good question. I guess she liked them. I never heard her say a word against either man."

"I meant why did they call the second husband Jack?"

"I don't know, honey. A nickname?"

"What was your mother's name?"

"Mary."

"Mary Tallack?"

"Yes. Her maiden name was Delroy, if that is where you're headed next."

"How long have you lived in Ilkeston Park?"

"I don't live there anymore, not for some time."

"How long did you?"

"Altogether? Geeze, I don't know anymore. Forty-five years?"

"We'll come back. How many children?"

"Did I have? Three. All of them delightful."

"What did you do for a living?"

"Your grandmother and I had a clothing store."

"What's your strongest memory?"

"That's a hard question to ask an old man, honey. After so many years there is no strongest memory. If you need something to put down say it was the day Kennedy was shot or when the World Trade Center was destroyed. And I suppose the day my wife died. That I recall like yesterday."

"What would you say is the key to happiness?"

Everyone laughed at the preposterousness of that one, even Abbie and she was only 17. Isn't it touching, the way we would all like to know?

"Detachment," Tallack replied.

"Can you elaborate?"

Diane interrupted.

"What's your theme, Abbie? What's your *theory*," eyes rolling in her head to signify passionate—it is hard to say what, *engagement* with this thought. "Otherwise," she said, "otherwise it is just the same old cobble. Rubble. History is piles of rubble. History at its pinnacle—do I mean pinnacle?—it is ordinary people."

"That is what Miss Boulanger said," Abbie told her. "'History consists in the everyday.'"

"Right again, Miss Boulanger. That is exactly where history gets going."

Johnny leaned behind Diane's head and whispered. All of them saw him do this. He put one of the lightweight summer chairs under Diane's backside and settled her into it. She quieted. She quit.

In nearly the same motion Johnny tipped more Scotch into his glass, this time with the generous hand of a drunk to himself.

"The vector of the gods," he remarked. "The best books I've read that were histories had no point of view. They weren't uncoupled, I do not mean that. But everything premises detachment, maybe to Pop's point, the detachment premise, a different angle—the better angles of our nature, you know, a different slice of light. In case you did not notice that was two clever puns."

"So you're not completely drunk," Dennis said in some sort of retribution for letting Diane have too much wine. All this just made Tallack tired.

"Can we finish later, honey?" he asked Abbie, knowing anyway she was glad to get back to the computer. "I'm tired now."

"Nothing is preordained," Johnny went on. "I can imagine, just for example, in a different version where I'm not a hard-drinking wife and father. My wife would like that, but then we would not be married. It is complex."

The sun edged the long shadows of the trees; the light was sweeter for the fat wet. Tallack was pleased to know the word for this: *lambent*. He recalled that "The Lambent Walk" was a dance craze when he was a youth. He could hear the tune in his head.

The way it will, the quality of the light restored lost time, though it was likely Tallack was cued by Abbie's questions. Once when Tallack was in the army he went to a pub in

Dorset, not far from the Hurn airfield, four of them—Syd Ballard, Cynthia and another guy, an American, Wallace Somethingorother. They took a table at the back of a pub. A trellis of spicy tea roses, the delicious sun of an English summer evening.

Lambent: good word.

Tallack recalled that Cynthia had a half pint of beer on the table in front of her. The sunlight bent through it to give her face the same ruby tint that Shelly's had in the instant she stepped through the back door with a big serving dish. One final bar of marigold light crossed Shelly's face when she came carrying a plate of peppers, onions and asparagus for the grill. She walked through the bar of light. Radiant. In that instant Shelly's face was radiant in the dictionary sense of returning light.

Endless interlocking. Given enough years, Abbie, all your memories will snap together like Lincoln Logs, fitted like a conspiracy theory of your own life.

Shelly swapped her plate for the cooked food and brought it inside. Dennis offered Diane his hand and they followed Shelly with their empty glasses. Eileen and Tallack were left with Johnny, who sipped his drink and smiled.

We have nothing to say to each other, Tallack was thinking, he is performing for us. My son is nearly 60 years old and he is not grown up. He still has no idea who he is.

At least there was the late-day bird song, pleasant as evening closed in, pleasant as the light went from the sky.

Lambent.

There it is, the at last.

Eileen's baby was born on June 17th. She named the child Siam. It was only a few weeks after the evening that Abbie interviewed Tallack for her school project.

Johnny phoned to tell Tallack the news of it. Tallack's eyes were welling the whole rest of that day. The next afternoon Dennis brought him to see Eileen in the hospital; Diane was somewhere else, Tallack did not know where. She did not go with them to meet the new baby.

At the hospital Tallack met the baby's father again—"Del"—now wearing the green dress uniform of an Army private. It had to be said Tallack was glad the kid got to see his son and he hoped no one thought it was taking sides to say so.

The other bed in Eileen's room at the hospital was empty and her friends sat on it. Eileen was the first of them to give birth, and they were amazed at this. Del stood at the foot of the bed holding the baby in his arms and grinning to beat the band while the friends who were there snapped pictures with their phones click click. Years from now those pictures of Del with Eileen and the baby will be misinterpreted by everybody. That is always the way it is.

Johnny and Shelly stood to one side of the merriment in that hospital room. They looked, it was difficult to tell what, *stunned* to see their baby daughter passed over into motherhood. The ruckus the friends made in the crowded room put them off, Tallack could see that.

Johnny flagged down a nurse from the hallway and told her the baby looked tired. The nurse got the message. She lifted the child from Del's arms and carried it off to the nursery.

Tallack followed the nurse. Looking through the glass he could not pick out one new baby from another. The room on the other side was half full of newborns—-pink and brown, hairless things like something just up out of the earth, not Tallack's idea of adorable. Fascinating, still.

"Siam" Eileen called the boy—yes, Tallack heard that correctly. At first Tallack thought Eileen had said "Sam." The child's name was her choice, and nice in a way, if the baby was a girl, but still nice, exotic, though Tallack was worried Siam would have a hard time of it once he started school.

Siam. Geeze.

Tallack was standing at the nursery window studying the babies when Johnny came down the hall with Del, presumably to give the boy a last look at the child he fathered. Del peered in at the babies in their plastic tubs and observed, "First there's nothing and then there's something." That boy was never going to be the brightest, this was certainly true, but the Army might make him into something plausible.

Then Del slipped his fatigue cap square on his head. He went off down the hall the way a movie actor with a war to fight goes off down a hall. Movies were probably how he learned to walk like that.

"Just don't forget where to send the checks," said Johnnie under his breath. He turned around to his father like he had made a good joke.

A moment later Shelly and then Abbie joined them. Tallack suspected they had been watching for Del to leave but he did not ask.

"Did you give Pop the package?" Shelly asked Johnny.

"I wanted Abbie to be here." Out of that damned shoulder bag he had started wearing Johnny took a fat envelope.

"What's this?"

"The biography of you I wrote," Abbie told him. "Ms. Boulanger gave me a B+."

"B+? Why didn't I get an A?"

"Part of the assignment was to show that we could work with databases. But with you there are gaps in the public record and some things I couldn't nail down. She dinged me for conjecture."

"Well I can't wait to read it, even if I already know how the story turns out."

"There're also copies of stuff I found when I was researching that I thought maybe you'd never seen."

"I can't wait to sit down with it. It is hard to imagine I can be researched."

"Everything's online somewhere," Abbie said.

Possibly it is not already obvious but Tallack was straining to be polite, and not just in a jokey grandfather's way.

Tallack's trips down Memory Lane had always been unmapped by facts and he did not welcome this pile of paper he was given. The heft of the envelope in his hand gave him the shivers, if you want to know the truth. It was like evidence in a case prepared against him.

Once they were home Tallack pretended to Dennis that he needed a nap. Sitting at the desk in his bedroom he tore open Marie's envelope. Initially things did not look so bad for him. Seen in isolation he appeared to be all in order, according to Abbie's essay.

> *Charles Tallack was born in New York City in 1924 the only child of Mary Delroy and Martin Dempster. Little and nothing is recorded in the databases about Mr. Dempster but it is known that he died in Mr. Tallack's infancy. After he passed on the mother was widowed. She later married Donald Tallack, for which Charles Tallack took his name as a little boy. Donald Tallack was known as "Jack," the reason for which is "lost to the past," according to Mr. Tallack.*
>
> *Charles Tallack grew up and married Marie Brochain from the Bronx, New York in August 1942. At the age of 19 he was drafted into the U.S. Army. During the Second World War he served in the United States Army for two and a half years in Europe.*
>
> *"When I got out of the service," Mr. Tallack declares, "I returned home to New York and started my family."*
>
> *Mr. Tallack earned his living working retail, owning a clothing shop in Ilkeston Park for more than 40 years. In his store of memories Mr. Tallack still strongly keeps in mind the famous "Pearl Harbor" attacks on the United*

States and the day his wife died.

"Even if you work at it," Mr. Tallack advises, "life is awfully hard. If you just accept this you will be all right. I think you will be happy. If you do not work at it I guess it does not matter what you do."

The secret to happiness, Mr. Tallack contends, is what he calls "detachment."

"Look at your life like it was a book you are reading or a movie you are watching," Mr. Tallack states. "You will see yourself more clearly and not get hard feelings involved over every little thing."

It is funny to read yourself quoted. Tallack understood why politicians were always issuing clarifications.

In Abbie's essay there was quite a bit to read, but tremendously little of it had to do with him. She was supposed to fill five double-spaced pages so she put in a lot of padding about historical events—the moon landing, the Suez Canal for Pete's sake—from all of which Abbie wrote that Tallack was "detached." Clever girl. To be fair, in his answers Tallack did not give her a lot to work with.

Abbie had found the death notice for Tallack's mother in the New York *Daily News* for July 16, 1945. Only four lines; you wonder why they bothered. In the newspaper they gave his mother's name as Tallack. On the death certificate issued by New York City she is Delroy. The certificate is witnessed by a coroner, Dr. Harlan Graves, who before then Tallack never heard of. Tallack noticed the doctor's name and thought "Graves" was a good name, given the man's job.

Tallack's Uncle Jimmy must have had a hand in placing

the newspaper notices and filing the death certificate—why would he let his sister die under two different names?

Our lives are full of pointless irritations that turn out to be something else altogether. Tallack did not say that to Abbie for her essay but it is true.

Two days after Siam (!) was born—which was a Tuesday—Eileen came home with the baby. Being a good grandfather Tallack called to say hello. But instead of Eileen (who was feeding the baby or something) Tallack's B+ biographer answered the telephone.

"Abbie, tell me," Tallack said, "how do you find things out?"

"There's websites."

"I don't know anything about that stuff."

"If a thing is public there is probably a way of finding it."

"Then tell me the key to happiness."

"Sorry, Papa?"

"I'm teasing. If we sat down together could you look up a few more things? That is what I would like to ask."

And for everyone's information, *that is* why Abbie was at Dennis and Diane's house on Tallack's last afternoon.

It was coincidence that Dennis and Diane decided to see a movie that day. They invited Tallack to come with them but he said no. Tallack had not been to a movie in years. He used to like going; he even appeared in one once and got paid good money for it when he did. Then one day he realized he could no longer follow plots. His head was full of too much else.

It was nice to have quiet in the house so that he could write down his questions for Abbie. All of them boiled down to when when when.

1. *When exactly did Martin Dempster die?*
2. *When did Mary Delroy Dempster (mother) marry Jack Tallack?*
3. *When she was in between husbands what was Tallack's mother doing in life?*

In the afternoon Abbie drove over. She had recently passed her driver's test and opportunities for taking herself places in the car were still a novelty.

"These are challenging," Abbie said when Tallack showed her his three questions. He leaned against the desk and watched her as she started to click click the computer in Diane's office. "They're versions of the same questions I couldn't answer for my report. The first place to look," she told her grandfather, "is the registry of births and deaths in New York. For each search they want a fee."

"I don't imagine there's a place to slide cash into that thing?"

"They want plastic."

Tallack was forever losing his wallet because he seldom used it and so he did not bother trying to find it. Going through Diane's handbag felt a little thievish but, were he still on earth, he would have pointed out that he kept a scratch pad of what he put on her card—$67—proving Tallack's good intentions right up to his end.

Anything to do with Jack, John or Donald Tallack came

up empty for the years they bracketed: 1922 to 1932.

"He doesn't have to be born in New York," Abbie said, "but didn't he die there?"

"You'd think I knew. Maybe Tallack was my mother's imaginary friend." Except that Jack Tallack bought an annuity that paid out when he died, and there are a few facts firmer than money.

"He could have died in a different state," Abbie offered. "Maybe New Jersey."

"That could be. He would still be just as dead, wouldn't he?"

Dempster's records, on the other hand, they found right away.

"Died July 11, 1924," Abbie read. "Cause of death is 'SI'. What's SI?"

"You tell me." Tallack's eyes hurt if he looked at the bright computer screen. Lately he was worried about cataracts. Of course he should have had that checked out but it does not matter now.

"The key at the bottom says 'SI' is the abbreviation for self-inflicted. Doesn't say how."

"Not what you expect to find."

"It does give us the place where he died. That might get us somewhere. 720 East 81st Street in New York."

"Ruthie's old address."

"Who's Ruthie?"

"My cousin or my aunt. I never settled on which."

"Now that we have a date and a place we can search death notices in newspapers from back then. That is how I found your mother's information."

"Try *The Daily News.* That's what all of them read. It is probably where her brother Jimmy would have placed it."

"Was Jimmy next of kin?"

"He was the family fixer."

Marie went up and down the computer for some time in silence and at last found a mention of Dempster. Not a mention but two full newspaper stories. The first one called Martin Dempster a "jilted Papa."

> According to Miss Dempster, her brother would not speak as he waited in her flat for his one-time heart's delight.
>
> "If my mother or me asked him even one question," said Miss Dempster, "Martin would just lift his finger in front of his lips. All he had to say was 'greed, greed, greed'."
>
> Some while later Miss Delroy arrived home with her infant. Apprised by a neighbor of Mr. Dempster's presence she relayed a message to her sister-in-law that she would not meet with her former husband.
>
> Hearing this, Dempster went at a gallop up the stairs to the roof. Deaf to his sister's pleas to withdraw he perched on its ledge for thirty minutes.
>
> "I looked up and thought it was just some man lost in thought," said Robert Darwin, who lives in the street and spotted the distraught Dempster on the roof's edge as he returned home from work.
>
> Police and a priest were at some point sent for. According to Fr. Daniel Brown, pastor at nearby St. Rita's, he and Dempster were deep in conversation on the roof when the grieving groom decided to try his wings.

"I'm midsentence," said Fr. Brown, "and then he shoved off, quick as a wink."

"Perched" the newspaper said, as though Dempster had become fishlike. Tallack knew the other meaning but in his late age he was easily distracted.

In front of his granddaughter Tallack was trying to remain, or appear to remain, detached, as if what he was reading had historical interest and that was it, nothing more. And so they sat like silent-movie actors, the pair of them, pretending not to look sideways at each other as they read.

"Look at the photo they published of your mother," Abbie said. "'Taken on her wedding day'. Your mom was gorgeous."

His mother looked like a little girl, that is what Tallack thought. The bride in the picture had no figure at all. Her wedding dress was cut as tight as anything women would wear 80 years later. The skirt was slightly higher than her knees. Her hair was clipped in what Tallack happened to know was called a "Dutch bob." She wore a juliet cap held to her head with a brow band; he recalled that Clara Bow used to wear those things in her motion pictures, or thought he did. For 1924 the outfit was daring; his mother was 19 years old and likely as interested in being fashionable as any girl her age.

The more interesting question, for Tallack, was who paid for such glamour? Reports of her father had him pegged for a skinflint. And he was getting the impression of Dempster as a bum.

"She's just a kid," Tallack said.

"Fashion forward though," Abbie said.

"She looks like Betty Boop," said the old man. In the girl's belly was him.

The two photographs in the *News* were muddy in the way of newspapers from those days. The other one showed Tallack's girlish mother startled by a photographer outside what he recognized as the front of Ruthie's building. Her features were washed out by the photographer's flash, her lips were apart in speech—what was she saying? "Help me?" "Leave me alone?" Clearly she was speaking, so what did the newspaper mean by writing "ashen silence"?

In this second picture his mother wears a dress with a wide stripe across the lower half. "Hobbleskirt": Tallack knew the word. And over her shoulder there was baby Tallack, his back to all the people, asleep most likely.

"I never knew mother lived with Ruthie. Ruthie always struck me as too eccentric for her."

"Did you know this story, Papa?"

"I knew part of it. I knew Dempster died before he should have. That's why my mother married again."

"How did you not know the rest of it? It's amazing."

"I guess they had the impulse to spare me the details. Parents spend a lot of energy reassuring children that everything's alright. Mother would probably have told me more about it some time if she had lived."

"I'm sorry, Papa."

"No need, honey. Honest, no need. It was a long time ago. Everyone's life happened anyway. Except for Dempster. What a stupid reason for killing yourself. But gee, my poor mother."

"We should read the other one."

"The other what?"

"The other one about your father." But it was not about Tallack's father. It was a Sunday feature all about his mother.

THE BRIDE STANDS ALONE

By Ruth Wheelwright

As the lady recalls, the moment was one from old-time melodrama. A frigid night in the Christmastide. Woman of the house, arrayed for bed, hears a rap on her door. On opening it she finds a shivering mother-to-be, shocked with cold, pleading homelessly.

Like all proper melodrama this one has a plot twist: the woman opening the door that night was the sister-in-law of the beseeching Madonna.

Ruth Dempster, the sister-in-law, has known Mary Delroy all of her life. They were kids together in Yorkville, not three blocks from where these events take place. About 18 months ago Miss Dempster observed her brother, Martin, take a sudden interest in Miss Delroy—freshly blossomed, it seemed to Martin, and all for him.

For the players in our show, 18 months was all it took for the whole world to turn over.

"Martin was kind of a galoot," says his sister Miss Dempster, who gives her occupation as educator. "He was my brother, I'll say that, but with people he could be sharp and at the same time dull—-sharp and dull. Mary took him by surprise, that is all I'll say. It was like he took a fit about her but it passed."

Miss Dempster sits on her sofa with her mother, Hilda Dempster, in their apartment on East 81st Street one evening recently while she relays a tale that ends with her brother's suicide last week.

The way she recollects, even as her brother's fancy for Mary Delroy gathered apace he was opposed by Mary's brother James, who has assumed the role of de facto pater familias, according to Miss Dempster.

"Jimmy's been the one," says Miss Dempster, an animated woman with an evident wealth of stories. "Their pop's all right but I think he's a hard case." She speaks of Mary's father. "From what I've met of him he's never around."

In defiance of Mary's brother, Martin Dempster courted Mary in secret. The way it so often happens when young people court in secret come spring the young lady in the story was with child.

A wedding was arranged for summer,

an annulment arranged for spring. By then Martin Dempster had three months left to live.

If this sounds like something out of Trollope or Hardy, the motor of our tragedy is altogether less exalted.

"Once Martin had Mary he lost his interest," in his sister's own words, who describes her brother as fundamentally a solitary sort. "I do not think he meant to be bad," she says, "but from a certain light you could say he was mean"—a comment that prompts her mother to lay a cautioning hand on her daughter's lap.

In December Mary's brother galloped to his sister's rescue and took her home to her family again. Dempster registered no protest. The annulment was filed, on what ground is unknown.

Enter a new actor

Except in melodrama it is uncommon for an expectant mother to find herself wooed by some new fellow. And yet the uncommon happens every day; there is irony in that but let it pass unexplored.

To Mary Delroy the uncommon kept happening.

Before autumn came Mary met Jack Tallack under circumstances neither Ruth

Dempster nor her mother will discuss—including whether Mary had by then removed herself from the home she shared with Martin Dempster.

But the women warmly recall a morning last November when Miss Dempster encountered a now visibly maternal Miss Delroy out walking with Mr. Tallack on Second Avenue.

"Mary was living with Jimmy and her father by then not even five blocks from us," says Ruth Dempster. "Our paths were bound to cross, what with everything. I did not expect her to be friendly or unfriendly," she adds in answer to a question. "Life has twists and turns, so who am I?"

Winter arrived and several more times Mary Delroy was encountered—including one memorable invitation to coffee with Mr. Tallack on a chilly Sunday when they collided once again at the local greengrocer. It happened that the elder Mrs. Dempster was along that day.

"I could see where Mary would prefer him to Martin," recalls the older woman, warmed by the memory of Mr. Tallack's fatal good looks. Compared with her late son Martin, she thinks, Mr. Tallack was fun, "but then they all are when they're after something."

Winter took hold of the city. Christmas loomed.

What the Dempster women could not know was that, however judged, what sweetness Mary had found was already soured. She had lost her best protector, her brother Jimmy, to marriage. Now she was on her own with her father, who never ceased to voice dismay at his daughter's missteps. The nightly scene in that house is easy to imagine. The quiets, the rages.

Worse, Mary was losing Mr. Tallack too.

"What she told me was that he asked her to the Christmas cotillion at his veterans hall," says Ruth Dempster, "which was all fine and good but for when he told her not to say they weren't married, that she should let people think it was his baby. She was showing by then."

As our scene plays out, it is Jack Tallack who, in a fit of candor that evening, mentions the truth to a fellow veteran's wife, the consequence of which is the eventual indignation of Mr. Tallack's mother, with whom he lives and who had been until then unaware of her son's liaison with Miss Delroy.

"The man blames the woman," says Miss Dempster. "Tell me something I don't know."

"He dallied with Mary," adds her mother.

In their few blocks of Yorkville Mary's new liaison was neighborhood news. Inevitably it reached the ears of Miss Delroy's father, who was escalated in his dismay. Unable to endure it longer Mary, on a night cold enough to freeze gin, wrapped her coat 'round her and fled to the Dempster house.

In retrospect, says Miss Dempster, "she was not expected."

Affections restored

Now is the third act of our tragedy. A baby is born (pictured), unencumbered. The bonds of affection among the three women are restored, helped out financially by two Dempster brothers in upstate Syracuse and by James Delroy. And by the baby's father.

"Martin (pictured) sent money," Martin's sister tells us. "But he showed no interest I saw."

A rapprochement of happiness or something like it reigned 'till last week, when on Friday Martin Dempster materialized at his sister's home, intercepting her on the return home from her job as an educator. He demanded to see his son.

The boy would never know his father's face.

According to Ruth Dempster, her brother

pushed in the door of her apartment and refused to leave.

Silently Martin awaited the return of Mary Delroy with her baby. But a kindly neighbor headed off the young mother, who fled then with her son, to where we will soon know more. Martin, on learning he had been bested, took himself to the roof of the building and leapt to his end.

The rest is just a headline.

What Martin never knew that night was that Mary Delroy had taken herself to the home Jack Tallack shared with his mother, remaining there since.

According to the Dempster women, our story will end this year with Mary's second wedding.

"Like it or don't," says Ruth Dempster, sanguine now, "Jack has the responsibility. Jimmy Delroy will see to him. Things will be better."

And the little baby boy?

"Mary will shape up," Miss Dempster tells us.

Tallack and Abbie sat, silent, until they were sure the other one had read down to the last word. There was no melodrama about it. Tallack sighed. He was only exhaling.

Tallack leaned back.

"What are you thinking, Papa?"

"That couch they were sitting on, the one the reporter talks about. I can see it in my mind. It was a cranberry color."

"But what do you think of what they're saying?"

"A mess. I think it was just a mess. But the mess that made me, right?"

"Seriously, Papa, you never knew any of it?"

"Until I was a grown man I did not even know Dempster was my father. Your grandmother told me, and I forget now how she found out. Even once I knew I assumed Dempster just died. People die, you know what I mean? Dying is normal. Which he *did* die but obviously I know now it was from what I could not have imagined him dying."

Tallack was awfully fond of Abbie. He was indebted to her now, notwithstanding that because of Abbie he knew things he did not like to know. He wished she would leave so that he could begin brooding right away.

"I recall an old lady," he said, "who lived with my Uncle Jimmy and Aunt Connie when I was a little kid. I always had a sense the old lady was not a relative to either of them. Now I'm wondering if that was Jack Tallack's mother, that maybe Jimmy made a deal with Tallack to take care of her. Ruthie makes it sound as if the two of them struck a bargain."

"Ruthie talks about your mother like she was brave."

"She may have been. She also may have been just another girl from the neighborhood who got pregnant and there's no more to her story than that. She could have been both. Nothing shameful in it."

"Eileen."

"Don't be disloyal to your sister."

"The whole time the reporter was poking fun at Ruthie,

wasn't she? Just letting her talk and then putting it all in the article."

"That's what they do."

"It wasn't nice."

"The way Ruthie was, even nice people had to fight the urge to be mean about her. She was a gossip and really an ignorant woman—ignorant as a savage. I mean it. But I have this idea savages are loyal, and Ruthie was loyal."

"Loyal to your mom over her brother, it sounds."

"She doesn't make Martin sound like much of a man, does she?"

"It feels like he was set up."

"How do you mean—set up by Ruthie?"

"By your mother."

"Pardon?"

"Sorry, Papa. I take it back."

"We're only talking, honey. No need to take anything back. Tell me."

"I'm almost the same age your mother was when all this happened and I feel like I've met her. All she wanted in this world was to get out of the house and away from her father."

"That's not uncommon."

"She got pregnant and that got her out of the house, what she wanted. But that didn't work out so she left Dempster and went back home again."

"Sounds like she had good reason to leave."

"According to Ruthie. But you just told me Ruthie was a big gossip. Sounds like she would believe anything anybody told her about Martin."

"I didn't mean to give that impression."

"People my age do it all the time."

"People my age do it all the time too. But when she left Martin my mother had to go back to her father, which is the opposite of what she wanted. According to you."

"Not for long."

"What do you mean—Jack Tallack?"

"This is what I'm thinking, Papa."

"My mother was not that calculating. Hardly anyone I ever met is that calculating."

"I'm not talking about calculating. Your mother could have been making it up as she went along. All I'm noticing is that by the end she got everything she needed. Everybody else ended up—what's the word? In the lurch."

"Except for me. What is 'the lurch'?"

"I don't know. Try to think of it like you don't know any of these people. We'll call your mother 'the girlfriend'."

"Do not make my mother sound like some kind of a tootsie."

"Like you said, it was 1923 and Mr. Tallack had a girlfriend what—seven months pregnant? He wanted everyone to think they were married, which now who would do that? One day he bumped into the pregnant girlfriend's old in-laws. That ought to be awkward. But instead the girlfriend says come have coffee. How did Jack Tallack feel? I would think he felt captured."

"You watch too many detective shows on TV. If they're your people you can't picture like that. Miss Boulanger would mark you down for conjectures."

"If I watched too many detective shows I'd make more out of the insurance policy…"

"…annuity."

"…annuity you said your Uncle Jimmy leaned on Mr. Tallack to buy."

"'Leaned on?' You make Jimmy and my mother sound like gangsters."

"Pressed upon him."

"You're a good granddaughter but about human beings you have the suspicious nature. You don't get all the way from your *conjectures* to the way my mother raised me by herself. It wasn't some big scheme of hers to leave the neighborhood and make off with the dough. She loved me."

Abbie was silent for an instant longer than Tallack liked.

"I'm sure she did, Papa."

The past is there, waiting.

"Hullo?" Tallack never knew it was so easy to place a call to England. Just pick up the telephone and ask an operator to look up the number of the person he wished to reach. The woman even put the call through for him. Cynthia answered on the second ring.

"Hullo?" she said again.

"Hello. Cynthia? Hello, this is Charles Tallack."

"Who's calling please?" Her voice was nothing like Tallack recalled. She squawked like an old woman. Man, that made him wince.

"It's Charles Tallack."

"Charlie Tallack? From America?"

"Hello, yes, that one. I was just here thinking about you and I thought to call."

"Well, how are you, Charlie?"

"I'm fine, Cyn. Like I said, I was thinking about you. And how are you?"

"I was only just getting into bed. It is *so* nice hearing from you, Charlie." Her voice downshifted. Down the phone came the small background sounds of whatever room she was in.

Tallack heard a wooden creak, Cynthia settling herself in a chair probably, sitting down in another country, not the one he was in.

"It's late there, isn't it? I forgot. I'm sorry to be disturbing you."

"Not at all, Charlie, you're not disturbing me. It is only odd hearing your voice. You sound the same."

"How are you, Cyn?" He seemed to himself to be insisting on an answer.

"Old, Charlie. I am very old."

"I've read about that happening to people."

"All these years you've never telephoned me. To what do I owe this nice surprise?"

"I just never thought of calling before."

"Charlie."

"To be honest and this will sound silly but I need to ask you a question. A question no one else in the world can answer." Tallack nearly said "no one left alive" but that would not have been flattering to Cynthia. "Except you," he added.

"After all this time you have only one question?"

Cynthia's reply distracted Tallack briefly before he said, "What I was a young man did I seem to you the sort of person who could not see the obvious?"

"What a question."

"It amazes me too."

"Do you want a yes or a no?"

"Today I'm ready for anything."

"You were sweet, Charlie. That is what I recall. I'll bet you are still. Are you, Charlie?"

"That could be taken for a yes."

"I don't know how else to answer you. You were stalwart." Tallack heard her talking, that was good, that was healthy for his mind, to make the voices in his head external, and to reply.

"Do you recall, Charlie, do you recall after Marie died you wrote to me something about having second lives or leading second lives, something like that? This would have been about seven or eight years ago."

"Of course I don't recall."

"Forgive me. But I have often thought about it since, what you said. More than once."

"If I *didn't* say that I like the way you express it. It fits the theme of the past few hours."

"And a few hours ago what happened?"

"I was looking over some old papers."

"Ooo, that is seldom a good idea, Charlie."

"It started me wondering if all my life I was missing what everyone else saw right in front of their face. In every regard I'm talking about."

"You are being a mystery, Charlie."

"Honest, honey, I don't mean to be."

"Calling me up out of the blue and asking philosophical questions."

"Forgive me."

"I telephoned *you* once, Charlie. Did you know that?"

"I do not recall."

"We didn't speak."

"That explains it."

"Your wife said you'd gone out."

"You spoke to Marie? My wife Marie?"

"Yes."

"I don't recall her ever mentioning it."

"We swore secrecy. If I thought about it I could even work out the year because the reason I phoned was that I was missing Bert after he died, so it would have been around then. I recall phoning on a Saturday when the rates were cheaper. Do you remember Bert?"

"Of course." Tommy.

"We were divorced 19 years when he died. And I was surprised to find I missed him. I began feeling I'd been mean to him, you see, in life. There was no one I could say that to who wouldn't tell me 'Well, *you've* left it a bit late, haven't you?' I telephoned you because I knew you'd never say that. But you weren't there."

"Apparently I was out."

"My impulse was to ring off immediately when Marie picked up, of course. But I thought, hang on, Cyn, you're not Charlie's mistress for heaven's sake, you live three thousand *miles* away. I know distance doesn't have to make a difference to another woman. Even I'm not that gormless. But it felt all right. We talked about you, of course."

"Why do women do that?"

"They don't always. I don't mean to say we discussed you at *length*. I said something to introduce myself, at this distance I can't recall what. We visited just like two old friends. She sounded like a very nice girl, Charlie. You must miss her."

"I mourn her. And how are you, Cynthia?"

"Keeping fit apart from the usual aches and pains."

"I had your last Christmas card. I thought you looked well."

"That was months ago, Charlie. Why are you really calling? Did you honestly not know it was my birthday today?"

"I should pretend that I did, but I did not. Happy birthday, Cyn."

"You're nice to remember."

"Now that I've reached you I can't say why I called. Maybe I just called up because I didn't want to miss the chance to speak to you again. I've thought a lot about you in life, Cynthia. I would like to say so."

"Charlie?"

"Yes?"

"That time I telephoned Marie said you'd just had a row."

"She did? It wasn't our routine to fight."

"She didn't tell me it was your routine."

"Did she tell you what we argued about? Do you recall?"

"Yes."

"Tell me or I'll never let you go to bed. I'll make you talk to me all night."

"Only because you insist. All the parties are gone now, aren't they? I don't see the harm." Tallack braced himself for harm.

"She said there was another man in her life."

"*That* harm."

"You asked."

"Go on."

"In her emotions, she said. But you know this, Charlie."

"I do not."

"Then I should stop."

"That would be cruel. Go on."

"Well, Charlie, she said the man was a university professor

of some sort who lived in your street."

"Please don't keep halting, Cynthia. The pace of this conversation is shortening my life."

"She said that she told you. That was my understanding."

"Cyn."

"Had just *told* you and that was why you'd walked out. She said it was… that she tried to tell you and you went out. This man, she said, *pursued* her for several years or more. Finally he asked her to run off with him. To Italy, can you imagine? The preposterousness of it was finally obvious to her. She told me she told you all this, I'm sure she did."

For one long moment Tallack said nothing, partly distracted by the unknown but probably shocking cost of a transatlantic phone call.

"I know nothing about it. I don't recall a fight. I certainly don't recall walking out. That wouldn't be me. It is missing from my memory."

"Oh well, maybe you had *not* had a row and I only filled that in on my own to make sense of why you were not at home. The whole time, Charlie, she loved you. I have no doubt of it."

Until Cynthia said that neither had Tallack.

"I love you, Charlie."

"I love you too, Cyn."

"Do you? Do you really?""

"I do. Had we not been married to other people and lived on different sides of the Earth I would have made a nuisance of myself all this time. But life is what it was."

"If I upset you then I am sorry."

"'Upset' is not the word. Is there a word for causing

someone else to become preoccupied?"

"*Entrance.* Do I entrance you, Charlie? Still?"

"Always. Forever."

"Charlie, some things will never be right. You know that. It is the way the world is."

"Yes?"

"Nothing to be done about the past."

"And isn't that a shame. I'm joking. It really is nice talking to you. Today I'm just tired."

"'Do not go quiet into that cold night.' Good advice, Charlie."

"Now we're started I know we'll talk more, Cyn," which they would not though Tallack was glad to say it and glad to hear it when she said back, "I would like that."

Even ears as bad as Tallack's heard the house tick. The very clean house. He felt he was going to jump out of his skin. This was the right way of naming the feeling. Exactly the sensation.

Tallack's eyes fell on a framed photograph of Eileen holding Abbie in her arms when Abbie was still a new baby. It was one of Tallack's favorites. Now the two little girls in the picture looked strange to him, as if they might be the sunny grandchildren of anyone at all.

Outside the air was heavy, Tallack assumed with oxygen. Good air for an old man. A colorless sky, neither this nor that. That evening it would rain or it would not.

Happily the church down at the bottom of the street was unlocked; Presbyterians are trusting people and Tallack never thought anything else. In the church he did not feel the solitude he felt in the very clean house, solitude so big it was finally really funny; the change of scene was already making a difference.

At that hour the sun was wearing down; the sky in the west was becoming the color of a blood orange, nice. Still the sanctuary was illuminated bright enough to read by. One light through many windows. The way it does at the movies before the show begins the light sank perceptibly, that thing of stillness and movement in the same instant. A trick.

Tallack was in a forward pew, right on the aisle, as if once the preaching started he would need a quick getaway. Fragrance of candle wax. Sleep could have come for him so easily.

It was sweet to be in the church dark, within the dark, within the warmth of stone walls. That week there was a lot of rain and the interior of the church smelled of damp; anyone could have grown mushrooms in there with very little trouble.

There was no reason at all to hurry home from the Presbyterians. After their movie Dennis and Diane were stopping out for supper. Dennis had offered to come collect him, to which now that Tallack thought about it he should have said yes. But beginning with that one Tallack swore off regrets.

Alen Tresca. Tallack did not know what to think about that. Mooning after Marie like a teenager. Delores was too alert not to know. All that time she and Tallack were friends Delores knew about it. Somewhere in some shoebox Tallack still had a snapshot of Tresca, good-looking in middle-age wearing sideburns and a sporty blazer, standing under a tree. The bastard. When Alen Tresca went to heaven what was he—maybe fifty at the most? If he died with a disappointed heart that was enough revenge for Tallack.

Here's what Tallack had that Alen did not: It happened once after Tallack was already married to Marie a long while. His kids were in the picture by then but that day they were somewhere else, Tallack could not have said where. Marie and he were in the kitchen cooking who knows what; all the detail is lost to the past. Tallack looked at her and in that instant she turned her eyes on him.

"Yes?" she said.

Tallack went to her at the sink and unbuttoned her dress. Marie never moved. Tallack inhaled her, her charming woman smell.

"Yes."

"Shall we ?"

"Turn the burner off."

Her breath on his face. Tallack could feel it even then, the warm breeze of Marie's breathing. In the bed Tallack consumed her. She was hips and breasts and all her flesh and her voice her voice her voice, how much Tallack missed her voice.

"Ruffle me."

After that they slept. On top of the bed in the warm daylight they napped naked. The intimacy of it was beyond words.

And that was not even the most memorable thing that ever happened to Charles Tallack.

What did his mother own that was anything like that joy, what was she ever greedy for? Tallack should have asked Abbie to look that one up. He did not think his mother was happy. She could never have been any other way but the way she was. Any other way never occurred to her. And what does one call that? A predicament, he supposed.

The creep of sleep was like watching the wind come across water: he knew the future.

Tallack was dreaming and he was dreaming about Marie. Here was Marie now, walking toward him near the stone wall of the church. She and he were outside the church in a place where big cars were not parked but were in some sense waiting, in some sense stuck in traffic. The grill of one intruded into the frame, like a dog nosing for attention.

This place was on the edge of a city and on a river. The surface of the river was chopped. It was the dead color of lead, the color before rain comes. Not the East River nor the Hudson but what other river could it be? What other geographies were settled so early in Tallack's dreamland?

People floated in a monochrome crowd on the perimeter of this place, people in their conversations and in their solitudes. They appeared not to see Tallack or Marie. Shelly and Abbie were fifty feet away and walking toward the river. Carrying a shopping bag by its handle Shelly walked to the river's edge and continued on. She waded in and began to swim toward mountains. (Jersey maybe?)

"Mama! Mama!"

Abbie was beside herself at being abandoned. She went into the water after Shelly, swimming until her strength surrendered. "Don't don't, honey!!" Tallack was shouting but neither Abbie nor any of the passersby heard him. Exhausted at last, Abbie floated back to Tallack on the current and collapsed in his arms, dripping, soaking his clothes. She did not speak.

Dennis was there looking at them. He looked like the saddest man in the world. All his hair was gone now.

Marie came back. Tallack was surprised that she was not more excited to see him. He was a little hurt by this.

Marie watched Tallack holding Abbie. It looked to Tallack as if she was not sure of what to do. He remembered that Marie never met Abbie. Abbie was strange to her.

"What happens here?" Tallack was conscious of the day's closing. The sky clouded.

"I don't have any idea."

"It isn't what I pictured." Abbie was gone.

"What would you like me to tell you?"

"I expected more resolution for people—explanation, a *place* of explanation. Like a college."

"Come on."

"Where is Abbie?"

"Life is what you make it."

"Where is Abbie?" The light was sinking. Tallack was really confused about it.

"This is dreaming. If you'll please just wait while I center myself and wake a little. I need to get this right."

"Shush," Marie said and she kissed Tallack, a big, surprising kiss and very welcome. It was such a long time since they had kissed.

"My father. My father died in a giant pout."

"Rest."

"He had no brains."

"Close your eyes all the way."

"He was unmanly."

"Shush."

"My mother."

"Shush." *Shush.* Good word for the… For how the day shuts down. It is precisely the sound of day's end, of the at last. Not for the hereafter, just for the at last.

Someone in a dark sweater was skating on a pond. It was ages and ages ago. Tallack had no idea who they were or what they were doing on his pregnant ponds of memory, his ponds.

At the back of his throat Tallack had the taste of mothballs. The Presbyterian church seemed to be filled with that scent. This was a puzzle to him, the last puzzle of his life.

When a long day ends it might still be regretted for not being long enough. With Charles Tallack that was how it was.

...and man, though idiotic, and knowing not what he does, yet full of the sweet things of love and gratitude.

Herman Melville
Moby-Dick

What feels promising is individual to us.

Abbie Tallack went to see her Uncle Dennis on the Saturday after her grandfather was buried. It was June of 2010. Summertime.

That Saturday was a wet one—"lousy" was what Abbie could hear her grandfather saying—and it was looking like a long day at home with her parents. Since the funeral they had been sniping at each other nonstop. Abbie's father had been insisting that she repay her Aunt Diane the money she and her grandfather charged for a records search on the day he died. They spent $67 on that. Aunt Diane told Abbie forget the money, she had "no earthly interest" in it; she said this as well to Abbie's father walking from the graveside. But her father would not let it go. It was about more than money for him.

On the street there was no place to park. All of her uncle's neighbors appeared to own at least three cars each. Abbie found a space a block away across from the Presbyterian church down there. Less than a week ago her grandfather passed away on a pew inside that church. Abbie liked the idea that his spirit might still be in there.

The sky was storm-colored. It was not giving up.

Abbie rang her uncle's bell. She looked into the big camera eye that watched her and waved at it. Standing on the front step she heard her uncle's heavy footfalls within the house.

Dennis beamed at the sight of his niece like a man in love. Abbie was 17 and to be so dear to anyone at all embarrassed her. She was a dark-haired girl lately growing into her face. She was hoping to be lean like her mother. She had been banking on that all through puberty. It still bothered her to have people look at her directly.

"What a nice surprise on such a grey day," Dennis said.

"Dad told me to call you first. I forgot."

"I didn't know it was raining," Dennis said. "Gimme your coat." For the first time Abbie saw some of her grandfather in her uncle's face.

"Rain's sort of stopped." Abbie fished out an envelope with a check inside for all the money and held it out to her uncle. "I came over to pay you the money Papa and I spent doing the records search."

"We talked about this."

"Daddy's annoyed."

"Annoyed about what?" Dennis sounded annoyed himself. His hair was thinner all the time in back but was resisting any turn to grey. Her father's hair was the same. Uncle Dennis was the taller of the two brothers by a full two inches.

"Because we borrowed Aunt Diane's credit cards to pay."

"If Diane wants the money she can sue Pop's estate. I'm making lunch—you hungry?"

In the kitchen a kettle whistled. Dennis lifted it off the gas burner and the kettle sighed itself to sleep. Abbie was reminded of a child spent after a tantrum.

The morning of the funeral Uncle Dennis bought seven pounds of cold cuts and other delicatessen whatnot. That was Diane's suggestion for after the service when people came back to the house. Dennis, Diane, Abbie and Abbie's parents were half of everyone who came. Aunt Maureen was living in Texas and anyway had multiple sclerosis for a long time; it broke Maureen's heart to miss her father's funeral but she could not do anything about it. After the funeral Abbie's sister Eileen went right home with her new baby to give him a nap. Anyone else who knew her grandfather and might have wanted a sandwich was either far away or dead for a long time.

From his refrigerator Dennis was removing a platter of meats that looked barely touched. He put everything out on the table without ceremony. Dennis was a low-fuss man and a pleasure to eat meals with. Marie's father was neither, or had become that way.

"You like roast beef?" Dennis asked her. "There's a surfeit."

"Turkey, please."

"Do me a favor and finish the pickles. The cole slaw is still good too. And oh," said Dennis, laughing as he sat down like someone making a good joke, "and *speaking of the estate* I need to talk with you and Eileen."

"About what?"

"Pop made me his executor. All his money and anything else of his you want belongs to you and Eileen."

Abbie did not understand the first thing about executors and estates; at her uncle she just looked back. She had no idea what he was talking about.

"It's not millions. Don't get your hopes up."

"I don't want Papa's money." Abbie's throat tightened the same way it did last Wednesday when her mother told her Papa was dead.

"Money is useful. No one's told you that?"

"Give it to Eileen. She needs it more than me."

"You don't need to decide today. You're not 18 and his will says I'm supposed to hold it for you. Talk to me in a couple of years. I know money's funny." Her uncle was smiling fondly at her. He found her youth charming. Naturally this was irritating to Abbie.

After three days the turkey was dry.

The pair of them ate in the dining room in an easy silence. Easy because it had the confidence of family connection in it; this feeling was a less familiar pleasure to Abbie than it ought to have been. Underlining their silence a clock in a walnut case that clicked on a side table like the tell-tale heart.

"Where's Aunt Diane?" Every house has its smell. The house of Uncle Dennis had a saturated smell of potpourri and scented candles.

"Yoga."

"Mom started yoga."

"She mentioned it. Would you mind if I ask you a question?" Abbie braced herself for a question about her father but that was not what Dennis asked about. "The other day—what were you and Pop searching for? I've been reading what you guys printed out. For the life of me I can't get where you were going with it."

"I can't tell you."

"Forget I said anything."

"I don't mean because it's a secret. I mean because I don't know. The two of us were trying out this, trying out that. Papa didn't really understand what a search engine is. He thought it was like a Magic 8 Ball, that you ask it anything and the Internet will know."

"I hope you don't mind but I read the printouts. Pop had them with him at the church. The cops gave them to me."

"Everything was in the public record." Abbie knew that much.

"They don't add up to anything. Pop already knew the basics about his father. I'm pretty sure he did."

Abbie thought for just a moment. She had eaten enough of the dry turkey to be polite and so now she said, "You know the way people say kids can't imagine their parents were ever young?"

"I have heard it said."

"Doing the search with him I could see Papa young. And I was thinking, 'I can see through time.'"

Dennis tilted his head, the universal gesture of bewilderment. Even dogs and cats do it.

"More of that, please."

"I don't know if he knew that it was his last day on earth

or what. But I could see he was trying to tie up loose ends."

"Did he say what kind of loose ends?"

"Not loose ends with his father. I think the father to him was just some guy who passed on his DNA. What do you know about Papa's mother?" Abbie heard herself speaking in the flat tone of a detective in a police procedural. She liked this role of investigator.

"Never met her," Dennis said of Tallack's mother. "She was dead before I was thought of."

"That's it?"

Dennis shrugged. "I have an idea my mother was friendly with her." Uncle Dennis had a little of the cole slaw on his chin. "Until you just asked me I forgot my mother even knew her."

"Did she like her?"

"If mom talked about her, yeah, I guess she liked her. To me she sounded kind of hard."

"'Hard' like mean?"

"Wrong word. 'Armored'. 'Durable.' You know? That was a quality people used to esteem."

"Was Papa?"

"Armored and durable?"

"I guess. Yeah."

"Sure. But I don't think people inherit their personalities with the DNA they get, if that's where you're going.."

"I'm not." On the contrary, Abbie was thinking of her own father, who waited until midlife to become a big drinker and now his face was all puffy. If that was her inheritance Abbie had no interest.

"Eye color you pass down."

"Sure."

"You want the printouts to keep?" Dennis asked.

"Don't you want them?"

"I might scan them just to have them, if that's alright. Pop would only have added them to all the paper he stored in his bedroom. He was like a branch of the National Archive. Send him a birthday card and he kept it forever."

"That's sweet."

"Be my guest if you want to dig through it."

"I don't picture Papa sitting down and writing people."

"As a regular thing he didn't. But he had a friend in England from the Army he used to write to. Pop kept all her letters from 1945 onward. Up until about a month ago."

"'Her'?"

"Nothing juicy, niece. Don't get worked up."

"Papa had a girlfriend?"

"Pop was married to my mother when he was drafted. And he was not the type to have girlfriends. But this woman—Cynthia Something—wrote to him a couple of times a year. I assume Pop wrote back."

"Your mother didn't mind?"

"She told us never to ask Pop about her. It was private, she said. We all kind of liked the idea that Pop had a second life. It made him more interesting. Mom didn't want us teasing him about it."

"What are you doing with the letters?"

"The other night before the funeral I burned them in the fireplace. I was fighting my curiosity and I had no right to read them. But I did write to the woman to tell her the news about Pop. That he died."

"How did you know her address?"

"I copied it off the most recent letter she sent him. She's old herself and at that age most of the news you get is that another friend of yours dropped dead. I hated doing it."

"Be interesting if she wrote back what she might tell you."

"Would you have wanted the letters?"

"No. You're right. They were private. You know what I *would* like one day?"

"Tell me."

"Someday can I have that photograph of Papa from when he was making the movie?"

Abbie was pointing at a framed photograph that sat on her uncle's long bookcase. It was a candid taken on the set of *Against All Currents* by someone in the 20th Century-Fox publicity department. It was the first day of filming and showed Charles Tallack waiting for the director to say "action." The picture was in a polished silver frame that set off the quality of the photo's blacks and whites. They were of a richness no one bothers with anymore. That photo had texture.

"Pop would be delighted that you want it," said Dennis. "*I'd* be delighted."

"Grandpa Jack has been putting white tape on the backs of things and writing people's names on them. He says he doesn't want arguments."

"Tell you what. I'll make a professional print from that one. You can have it now instead of waiting around for me to keel over. That would only make me nervous."

Abbie looked at the photo again and already felt the pleasure of possession. It showed her grandfather at 34, not as the old man she had always known. He was handsome in his crisp pleated trousers and tailored jacket. Papa had a strong face, Abbie thought. He was about to walk into the first shot of *Against All Currents.*

From the look in his eyes Abbie imagined she could read what her grandfather was thinking. Probably trying to recall his two lines of dialogue. Uncle Dennis once told her how her grandfather was supposed to leer at Helen Darrow's backside as he walked down the street but he made up his mind not to do it no matter what the director wanted. Abbie also knew that her grandfather was fighting a summer cold and a fever that day. She heard the story lots of times.

"Papa looks like he's all business," said Abbie. "You know?"

"It *was* all business. They always needed money."

The photo was amazingly crowded. By Tallack's feet a cameraman sat on a kind of sled at the top of a short length of track, waiting to make his shot. Meanwhile other crew and some neighbors from Ilkeston Park—all of them White women but for one Black man and all of them dressed up in a way people don't trouble with today. They crowded around the edge of the set behind a wooden barrier. Abbie's grandmother, the woman for whom Abbie was partly named, stood not quite directly behind Tallack, pleased about him to judge by the little lift of her mouth.

Looking amazed are Uncle Dennis, Aunt Maureen and her father. They were all just children then. Papa was the anchor of their lives. They were the anchors of his.

To see them all so young just fascinated Abbie. The sky was platinum above their heads.

So promising.

Then it was 2025.

Every Saturday evening since the dark winter months Abbie and her daughter Joni took the M79 bus across Manhattan to the Yorktown Aquatic Center. Those two evenings a week Joni's school team swam laps for an hour.

Abbie savored the time on the bus with her daughter, savored the noise at the pool of splashing kids and their crazed laughter. Abbie knew how whole years moved fast. Sooner than Abbie could have imagined Joni would be grown and gone, quick as a wink.

Lately Joni was making a statement of wanting to walk into the facility on her own, without her mother. Abbie conceded the point; it was the right way for Joni to feel. Just the same, Abbie—midsized and fair, and what with this and that looking older than her 32 years—stood on the other side of the YAC's doors watching her tall eight-year-old, already building a swimmer's broad shoulders, swept away in the current of kids.

Joni never knew that her mother watched. Joni never looked back.

On Saturdays Abbi went for dumplings down on the corner of 1st Avenue.

That evening it was raining, a suitable June rain, steady and light. Abbie put her umbrella up and walked west. Her routine was to visit a Chinese place on East 81st Street, Café Bàng. There she passed an hour eating shrimp shiu mai, watching the street and talking to her mother on the phone.

Johnny Tallack was dead; no surprise there. He never did anything to take care of himself so what did he expect? For 15 years he had been rehearsing death. Eventually he stopped drinking. This was not from any decision he made but from illness; that was what it took. Right to the end the women in Johnny's life—Abbie, her mother Shelly and her sister Eileen—all jollied him. None of them knew another way to be and so they let it play out.

To his credit, Johnny knew to appreciate the love he was getting at the close of his life. He said thank you out loud to Shelly and his daughters. But he died without contentment. Revelation never came for him. To daily miracles Johnny was obtuse.

Abbie once asked Shelly, "Why did you stay married to daddy?" That conversation was four years ago, long enough after Johnny's death that the three women who survived him had acquired a little detachment. "Just for the record," Abbie told her mother, "Eileen and I would not have objected, if that's what you two were worried about."

"I'd like to tell you it was a decision," Shelly answered, "but the thought of ending a third marriage was just more exhausting to me than staying in a difficult situation. I never even tried on the idea of divorce. So if you're wondering I was not being brave."

"Not love, then?"

"Love, sure. Sure. That and the low energy for it, let's be honest."

Shelly still lived in the house where Abbie grew up. Recently she found a new fella, Dominic Caravello. Dominic was the father of a boy Shelly taught one year early in her teaching career. (The "boy" was now a 41-year-old electrical contractor working out of Ilkeston Park.) Dominic recalled Shelly from parent-teacher meetings. Even before Johnny died Dominic used to chat her up when he met her around town, reminding her of how they knew each other. When at length Dominic's own spouse died, quite a nice woman according to him, he got more assertive in his friendliness. He was forward, to use Shelly's phrase.

Now Abbie's practice when she went for shiu mai was to telephone her mother and get the latest. She had no idea how interested her mother was in this Dominic except that for several months they had been going to movies and other entertainment whatnots. "Dominic is social," Shelly said. "He likes to go places, so we go." When they spoke the week before Shelly told Abbie they might take a package tour to Aruba in August, which is the off-season when the prices are cheap.

"You'd share a bed?" Abbie asked. Her mother laughed out loud.

"My goodness, Abbie. You sound so afraid of scandal—how were you raised? I'm **71** years old. If we go, yes, we'd share a bed."

"Wow, ma. You're sporty."

Shelly was happy now. She was light of heart. When her father was alive Abbie never knew her mother to be light of heart.

After Johnny died Shelly went on teaching at the high school. She did so chiefly for the stabilizing virtues of routine while she worked out a next act in her life. When she retired at 70 she remarked to Abbie, "I surprise myself by how strong my body is. Good genes, I guess. I might live a long time."

"Ma, you've been ruminating."

"I'm only curious," Shelly said, "to see what else the world might still have for me. You know?" If Shelly meant to have a second life and if it included Dominic Caravello then Abbie was all for it. If anyone was asking.

Speaking to her mother Abbie watched the street out the café window. She was looking through a painted red dragon with the world in its mouth.

"Right this minute a man is walking his dog past my window," Abbie told her mother. The man and his dog were taking their sweet time, letting the suitable rain just come down. The man wore a Boston baseball cap.

"How old?" Shelly asked her.

"Seventy maybe. I'm guessing. Pretty good-looking guy, ma. Your cohort."

"Run outside and get his phone number. Tell him if things don't work out with Dominic I'll be in touch."

Once Abbie heard a lady on TV say we grow up to be one of our parents and marry the other one. It was the sort of clever thing to say that falls apart on two minutes' reflection.

Abbie thought she was like neither her mother nor her father. She would say the same of her husband, Anthony. He sold all varieties of insurance and he was even-tempered and direct. He was a dark-skinned man from Ohio, the son of two dentists. In other words, he was nothing at all like Johnny Tallack. Anthony was kind, which in his life Johnny often forgot to be.

Neither was Anthony like Abbie's mother, for all Shelly's qualities. Watching her with Johnny in his last two years Abbie started thinking Shelly was maybe not so easy herself in the day-to-day of marriage; Shelly was dutiful but in a way that had something latently belligerent in it.

If Anthony was like anyone he was like Abbie's late Uncle Dennis, but that was pushing the analogy so hard it broke.

The year before this time Abbie went for a mammogram. A lump was discovered in her right breast. After she was diagnosed she spent too many months in this neighborhood where she now ate dumplings. About ten blocks south was the office of her cancer doc. Nearly every week Abbie visited specialists, getting tests, having biopsies. Through all of it she was more ticked off than frightened.

Cancer Abbie hated. She did not discover uplift in disease, no divinely devised revelations. Cancer was cruel and that was all. Chemotherapy made her sick. Her face—even her ears—puffed out from the chemicals. Cancer cost her any chance of having a second child with Anthony.

So far Abbie looked good for recovery if the radiation and the five years (!) of hormone therapy worked as advertised. Abbie was not armored. But she was durable.

Anthony was beside her the whole way, at chemotherapy every three weeks, at all her blood tests and biopsies. Before chemotherapy started Anthony went with her to a salon to get her hair cut off. "I don't want it falling out in clumps like I had the mange," Abbie had told him. After the haircut Anthony brought her to a bar she liked and held her while she cried; he knew not to say one single word.

When Joni took the test for the BRCA gene Anthony went too.

"If it's inherited from me," he told Abbie, "I need to look Joni in the face when she learns she has it."

"You're a paragon," Abbie teased him, "but we don't have charge of our genetics. That's a roll of the dice."

"It doesn't feel that way if it's your own daughter. It can't."

Before she was sick Abbie might go more than a month without speaking to her sister Eileen. With an adolescent son and a job, life barreled along for Eileen with her son Siam, the same as it did for Abbie.

Eileen was making her living as a realtor. Selling real estate was a surprising career choice; Abbie found it hard imagining Eileen being easy with people for a job. Not to unsay any of that, but once she heard Abbie was sick Eileen started phoning a couple of times a week, usually for no reason at all.

Eileen volunteered to be Abbie's escort for the treatments; she lived not three blocks from the hospital. When Abbie told her she had Anthony for company Eileen looked at her funny. Anthony and Eileen were always prickly with each other for reasons Abbie did not know.

Eileen did not inherit the gene for marriage the way Abbie did.

The day Anthony took Joni for her BRCA test overlapped with the third of Abbie's chemo treatments. Eileen went with Abbie in Anthony's place. That evening Anthony asked how was it.

"I threw up after," Abbie told him. "That was nothing to do with Eileen."

"You got along?"

"We always get along. She sat with me very nicely while I vomited and I was thinking of how she used to be my hero." Which words were no sooner out of her mouth than Abbie wondered if they were ever true.

As kids Abbie and Eileen were five years apart. Their circles did not overlap. When Eileen came home from college pregnant Abbie was old enough to be exasperated with her. On that subject Eileen got enough exasperation from Johnny and Shelly, so Abbie kept quiet. But she was, she was exasperated.

Another thing was that, alone among her family, Abbie believed Eileen was mean to Del, her son's father. Not that Abbie had affection for Del; no one had affection for Del; that was too difficult to manage. But Del was never late with a child-support payment or a birthday card to Si. (Siam was thank God rechristened "Si" the moment he began preschool, probably to the kid's relief.) Except for two weeks in summer when Eileen was obligated Del never saw his son. He did two tours in Afghanistan and in those years did not see his son at all.

Abbie wondered about the messages Eileen was sending Si in the way they lived. Messages about romance (don't go near it), about men (of which Si with his dark stubble and froggy voice was clearly one) or about happiness in general (enjoy it when it passes through but don't overinvest).

Abbie presumed it annoyed Eileen that as Si grew up he looked like his father and not anything like a Tallack or a Siperstein. Si was tall the way his father was tall and had the same poor posture; 15 years old he was already beginning to loom over his mother, aware of his swaying height. Lacking his father's bravado Si made one worry for him.

One time when he was about 12, about the age to begin noticing what was peculiar about his household, Si said to his Aunt Abbie, "She never goes out at night. I don't even think it makes her lonely."

"She's got you."

"It's not the same thing."

"Maybe she just doesn't show the way she feels about it."

"Mom shows everything, Aunt Abbie. She thinks she doesn't but she does. I never see her needing company."

"I'm in your corner, Si." It was the best Abbie could manage. She wished that once he was old enough some circumstance would arise to get Si out of Eileen's house and geographically far away.

After that time Eileen went to chemo in his place Anthony suggested to Abbie that she ask her sister to be her regular chemo partner.

"When you throw up she can hold the bucket as well as

I can. You'd be giving her something if you let her keep you company."

"Aren't you Mister Fix-it." Anthony was wrapping her legs in cold compresses as they talked. Sometimes for days her body sang painfully with a kind of electrical feeling.

Abbie used to schedule chemo for seven a.m. in case she felt well enough after to go to work, which about a third of the time she did. Beginning in October she and Eileen met in the predawn dark on York Avenue and went in together. Afterward they visited a coffee shop nearby, not for breakfast (most days Abbie could barely keep down plain toast) but because coffee shops had bathrooms into which Abbie could dash if she felt sick. Breakfast was pretense.

Over one of these breakfasts their grandfather came up in the conversation and Abbie said, "If Papa could see us now I would want him to be proud of us."

"You think he worried we'd grow up to be embarrassments?"

Abbie was taken by the sharp tone in Eileen's voice. Eileen held grudges (like Shelly, to be honest).

"It was just a thing to say."

By the end of March Abbie's old greed for life was coming back. Her hair was growing again. She had not liked being bald (she had vanity the same as anyone) but most of all she hated the way her skull that winter was cold all the time. Her collection of colorful kufis could not change that. The being cold was one more reason Abbie was glad once June came.

At six thirty on a Saturday evening traffic was light. On Abbie's side of the café window cars and trucks made sounds on the wet street that she heard and she did not hear.

On the other side of the glass, the side where the world was, a man about 30 walked past holding a little girl with one hand and carrying three green bags of groceries with the other. Beyond them a soaking-wet bicyclist with iodine-colored hair swore at a man driving a bread van when the van stopped short. The owner of a pharmacy pulling down the metal gate of his storefront turned to look when he heard their obscene back and forth.

At the corner a couple kissed. They looked probably older than Abbie and Anthony. They ignored the swearing of the breadman and the red-headed cyclist. The man had a suitcase and a duffle he put into the trunk of a cab. The woman kissed the man again as he climbed into the taxi. She stood on the corner watching him disappear up First Avenue before turning away and walking offstage.

Little dramas everywhere.

Whenever she was in Yorkville Abbie was distantly aware that this was the neighborhood where her Papa grew up. Should he return from the dead Charles Tallack would see little to trigger memories of the old life, little trace of the East 81st Street he knew. New York has always been this way, erasing the scenery—people's backdrops—and redrawing it again. The whole city is pentimento.

Abbie knew roughly where Ruthie Dempster's home would have been; she knew because on a morning the previous November she made a project of finding it with Eileen. She was feeling chemo-brained that day and thought walking in the cold fresh air might blow the clouds from her head; that was the image she had. Whether it did or not (Abbie was sick once into a street-corner trash bin) they located where Ruthie's and probably two or maybe even three other walkup apartment houses used to be.

Now the physical space of those ghost buildings was filled entirely by one luxe condominium. Its doorman kept an eye on the two sisters peering at them from out on the sidewalk, the shorter one of them wearing a particolored knit cap on her head.

The sisters found the doorman's suspicious nature funny. This was a nice moment for them.

They tried to guess the spot where Martin Dempster, their great grandfather, hit the pavement when he leapt from Ruthie's roof. There was nothing to see except in their imaginations. The sidewalk since that evening Dempster pushed off had been ripped up and replaced who knows how many times since the day Dempster dented it.

At home Abbie still had the printouts about Dempster in the same big envelope Uncle Dennis gave her nearly 15 years before. Now and then in a search for something else she came across that envelope among all the other paperwork that goes with her grown-up life. The paper was crispy and yellow with age; that is what Abbie noticed. So was the biography of her grandfather she wrote in senior year of high school, the one for which she was given a B+ because of conjecture (a miscarriage that will irritate Abbie until the day she follows all the rest of them up to heaven).

In the months when she was most sick Abbie worked on her point of view about dying. This was to be expected after the idea of being dead became more than theoretical. Abbie concluded that she would prefer not to go out like her grandfather, canted over in a church pew like someone having a nap during a bad sermon. People commonly say nodding off like that is the best way to die, death coming for us on tiptoe. Abbie's opinion was that she liked life and hoped she would be given a chance to say the right kind of goodbye to it.

Abbie understood she had no clue what it felt like to be as profoundly old as her two grandfathers when they passed on, so inexpressibly old. She did not know what it was like to say "enough" and not have the whole world treat that statement as a psychosis, something to be cured—like cancer, to make the obvious analogy.

The blameless rain continued. Behind the wide window Abbie was dry, watching the street through the dragon painted on the window of Café Bàng.

The traffic noise seemed to switch off. Yet life in the street was going on just the same. The switch to silence was abrupt enough that Abbie looked up.

From the west side of Manhattan long wet light now poured into the avenue just behind the curtain of rain. The wet streets gleamed sort of magically. The sky was the palest blue. The evening was warm and red and unhurried.

Summertime. Urban summertime.

So promising.